Rheged: A Tale of Pilgrimage

D0514476

To my family.

~ Chapter 1 ~

"We have a fine selection of weaponry prepared for Your Highness." Aelhairn Urien was being escorted to the royal armoury of Wetherstag, the capital city of the Kingdom of Rheged. It would be the first destination upon his return, for, according to tradition, a king without a sword was no king at all. "The best swords in the land, from the Helm to the Clovenstone – you'll find them here." Urien's servant, whose diminutive stature was offset by an impressive paunch, continued to wax lyrical about the quality of the equipment that awaited them. Urien, however, was absorbed by the view from his carriage window. The blotched heifers, furrowed fields, and distant hills all evoked a faint recollection of a contented past; but Rheged was a more peaceful country then, and the closer Urien's carriage came to the city, the less he recognised. Forlorn expressions, beleaguered gestures, indignant voices – this war-weary place was a far cry from the proud kingdom that he had left a half-century ago.

Urien's reverie was terminated as the carriage jolted over a tree root. The convoy had reached the colonnade of oak trees which graced the final length of the King's Road – the same trees, the same road, which had marked the beginning of his pilgrimage. As the sturdy trunks stood to attention, the motherly branches sprinkled the morning sun onto the dusty road, celebrating his arrival just as they had mourned his departure. Through the tunnel of leaves and limbs, which formed ever-new arrays of shadow and sunlight as they swayed serenely in the late-summer breeze, Urien caught a glimpse of the city's white ashlar walls.

Built by the Old Fathers themselves, they had decayed with time, and now displayed only a trace of the glory bestowed on them by those first, great kings of the Old Kingdom of Rheged.

The retinue proceeded through the city gates without interruption, the iron portcullis falling thunderously to the ground behind them. Inside the city, Urien was struck by a mixture of energy and enervation. The townspeople were single-mindedly engaged in their various vocations, yet they displayed an almost defensive stupor, a refusal to be fully awake, as if they could no longer bear the burden of reality and yet had no other choice. As they lumbered along the chock-a-block streets, hauling sacks and pushing carts, they seemed to count each and every cobble, as a prisoner might tally his days. The city had truly changed – and so too had Urien.

Inside the armoury, the glum commotion of the street was concentrated into a furnace of exertion. Urien was directed to a collection of swords exhibited sacramentally above a velvet-draped rostrum – the king's own arsenal. Speculatively, he lifted the item which most brashly vied for his attention – a resplendent, polished blade with a gold-plated crosspiece and a jewel-encrusted pommel. At once, the cacophony of clanging metal from hammer, anvil, sword, and shield, the commotion of garbled voices from bellowing commands and boorish conversations, the clamour of hooves, grunts, and whinnies from obstreperous horses, all settled to an unnerving hush. No one but the king dare touch the weapons on that wall, under pain of death. This frail, antiquated stranger could only be the king himself, come to restore his reign.

Urien could sense the fixation of expectant eyes; but the object felt foreign, awkward, and unduly heavy in his arthritic hands. Though he knew not what qualities he sought, he was certain that they could not be found in this vain decoration. He replaced the weapon before sampling several more, only to discard each of them amid mutters of anticipation. On his journey, Urien had found true treasure, true riches, true value. The trinkets on the wall were mere imitations, travesties even, designed merely to posture and impress, to distinguish ruler from ruled and to conceal weakness and failure behind a semblance of majesty; his sword would not be found here. Urien stepped down from the platform to groans of disappointment before the bustle of the armoury tentatively resumed.

The dwarfish servant who had eulogised the arsenal began deliberating with Urien. "Perhaps we could revisit the vaults – some of the lower chambers may have escaped our search. Or perhaps we could have one forged for Your Highness." Urien, though, was looking across the armoury. The patterns and rhythms of the place seemed to reverberate in a deserted chamber of his mind, a hidden vault of past and future. As he groped to trace the intimations, he noticed a hoary blacksmith, crouched over a basic workbench, executing his work with unwavering concentration. The diligent veteran belonged to the same bygone era as Urien, and betrayed the same out-of-place aloneness. Urien began to stroll casually across the room, attempting to camouflage himself in the to-ings and fro-ings from which the craftsman seemed uniquely withdrawn.

Arriving at his destination, Urien stood in front of the blacksmith's table. "Highness," the blacksmith murmured drowsily, without looking up from his tools. After waiting in vain for the old hand to afford a gesture, Urien sat down on a nearby anvil. "You need a real sword," the blacksmith averred with the same muffled inertia.

"Begging your pardon?" Urien replied, startled yet curious.

"Them swords ain't for fightin'. Them's for lookin' at."

Urien suppressed his agreement, still sizing up the man. "What would you suggest?"

The blacksmith held up a mended horseshoe to inspect it in the light. For the first time, Urien saw his eyes – solid white, without iris or pupil, like perfect pearls.

Satisfied with his handiwork, the cataracted farrier added the horseshoe to the appropriate pile. Without pause, he reached underneath his bench to produce a sooty, unremarkable sword and scabbard. "Highness," he droned as he slid the weapon in Urien's direction, his drooping eyes once again concealed.

Urien hesitated to accept the donation until he noticed the pommel, which had been forged into the shape of a crown. In all his days, he had only ever seen one sword with such a feature; and that sword had long since passed from this world. His incredulity vanished as clasped the splintered hilt: it fit his palm like a bone in its joint, as if it were an extension of his body. As he unsheathed the lacklustre blade to reveal its faded engravings, he remembered. Yes – Trusmadoor – this was his sword.

~ Chapter 2 ~

Bedwas Owein gazed soberly into his porcelain teacup. Drained of their vitality, the fragments of leftover tea leaves had gathered in a mass grave at the bottom of the vessel, as if they had already accepted their fate, as if they longed to finally rest in peace. In a bid to revive the fallen particles, he carefully churned the cup to induce a gentle eddy. The lifeless dregs followed the force of his hand in pitiful submission, only to capitulate the moment he abated, resigning themselves again to the murky depths. He clasped the artefact in his palm, remembering the warmth that once emanated from it. Elegant but delicate, he imagined that it would break if he held it but a little harder. He stroked its smooth frame as if to console a loved one – as if he were its father, the potter who had affectionately shaped it into existence.

This brittle relic was his country, the crushed residue his people; but he was not their father. Their true father, his own father, had long since abandoned them. Driven by some delusional vagary, some fanciful notion born of desperation or planted in his mind by one of his devious advisers, Aelhairn Urien had embarked on a senseless quest to restore the Ancient Way of Dalriada. At only twelve years of age, Owein had been left to rule the Kingdom of Rheged – to enforce its laws, to control its coffers, to wage its wars. He had inherited a kingdom long in decline; and, alas, he had been unable to stem the tide. What had Urien expected? What madness had driven him to elope with his fantasies and leave a boy in charge of the Kingdom, aided only by a cabal of conniving councillors? And why had he now returned?

Urien was due in the throne room, where Owein now awaited him. Owein could not recall his father's face, which would anyway have changed over these long years. Indeed, he had tried his best to eradicate all memory of Urien, presuming, along with the rest of Rheged, that he had perished somewhere in the wilderness. Until her own death, Owein's mother Coira had assured him that his father was alive, that he was fulfilling a sacred duty, and that he would one day return. She seemed to know more than she disclosed about her husband's truancy; but eventually Owein conceded to the consensus that she had merely lost her mind, tragically following in the footsteps of the one whose fate she could not bear to accept.

Owein's attention returned to the practicalities of his present situation, for which the traditions of Rheged made no allowance. Was he to yield the throne to his father, who had never truly abdicated? Or was he to assert his own claim, though he had still not received a sword of kingship? Did he even want to be king? Did Urien?

Finally, Owein heard a clip-clop of hoof on cobble followed by a shrill chink of armour and mail. The royal entourage had arrived. Owein suddenly felt out of place seated on the throne; and as the sentry delivered three purposeful knocks against the solid oak doors, he could not prevent the hair on the back of his neck from standing to attention with the guards. The crown on his head felt heavier than ever, like a manacle for his mind.

"Come," Owein uttered coldly, swallowing the apprehension in his throat. As the doors heaved inwards, he felt his own insides heave, as if the sunlight that breached the chamber was exposing his nakedness. A solitary silhouette appeared at the threshold. "Come," Owein repeated, according to the custom.

As the great doors rumbled shut, the figure that stepped forward was transfigured into Aelhairn Urien, the lost king of Rheged. He was older, to be sure – his beaming face had wilted, his golden locks had whitened, his strapping frame had withered. Yet this was still Urien, and Owein recognised him as if it were forty years past. Urien proceeded across the hall and knelt at the tribune on which the throne was perched.

"Highness," he hailed deferentially, averting his eyes.

Although Owein had memorised a formal address, his tongue was tied between exultation and resentment. He fumbled for something to say; everything seemed inappropriate in one way or another.

"Father," he finally blurted, his voice cracking with ambivalent affection.

Urien looked up to the base of the throne, and then to Owein. "Son."

Owein's defences began to fail. He yearned to spring from his throne and embrace his father, who was dead, but now alive again; who was long lost, but now, at long last, found. Owein was at the point of surrender when he was saved by a familiar trio of wooden thuds. "Come," Owein commanded. Realising the significance of his action, he glanced demurely at Urien, who, by contrast, was fixated on the entryway; he knew that only an emergency would warrant such an intrusion. Aping his father's sternness, Owein issued the second command before the doors had fully opened. A courier stepped in timorously from the sunlight.

"Begging your pardon, Your Highness – Your Highnesses," he stammered. "I bring tidings from the eastern front." The messenger paused, uncertain as to which king he should address.

"Well, go on!" Owein clamoured from across the hall, irritated more by the hesitation than the interruption.

"The Helm has fallen, Your Highnesses," the courier spluttered. "Reinforcements have been sent to Ravenshield but the Qa are pouring into the strongholds. We expect to lose the whole range by nightfall."

Urien looked to Owein, who was too ashamed, too inhibited by the pressure of sonship, to meet his father's gaze. "Bring me the High Commander immediately," Owein snapped. "And ready an emissary. That devil of a king Dunragit has something to answer for here."

~ Chapter 3 ~

Bassien Dunragit, King of Durdich, was pacing across his throne room. A near replica of Rheged's Great Hall, the room was differentiated by its indigo draperies and silver tassels – a deliberate picture of the Birch of Ibar, the emblem of Durdich's sovereignty, set before the vast waterbodies which riddled the land. A bonfire was burning in the hearth; yet its red light and gold heat seemed to dissipate immediately into the solid sandstone walls.

"Your Highness, the Helm has been taken," crooned an obscure figure from a dim corner. "We have Owein by the scruff of his mangy neck. It's only a matter of time before Ravenshield falls to the Qa – and after that Wetherstag."

"And what then, Beggerin?" the king replied distantly, pausing his patrol. "What will be your strategy for fighting Aram on two fronts?" He turned to face the fire, his intonation becoming more direct. "And what's to say that we won't be next?"

The wraith emerged from his shadow to reveal a formless lump of a man, his face a lunar landscape of craters and protrusions, his back a crooked crescent. "With the utmost respect, Sire, the Qa have no appetite for conquest." The goblin began hobbling toward the king, employing a steel cane that remained concealed under his baggy cloak, striking the marble floor with sharp, metric knocks. "They mean only to shore up their borders, to act on Rheged's weakness and ensure that Aram lies beyond its grasp." When Beggerin stopped, the percussion of his cane echoed faintly throughout the chamber. "We are more ambitious," he continued. "Only when the Empire is routed once and for all will Durdich be free from the yoke of oppression that has afflicted this country since Brackentrod."

Dunragit flinched at the mention of that infamous battle, in which Durdich's age-long rebellion had been definitively crushed, its people condemned to remain under the dominion of the Empire. To be sure, much had transpired since then – the interminable war with Aram had taken its toll on Rheged, which had gradually withdrawn its forces from the outer provinces. Durdich had eventually crowned its own king, Ibar Drochduil, and established its own capital at Mallerstang – the city where Dunragit, Drochduil's great-grandson, now reigned. Nevertheless, the wounds incurred at Brackentrod had not healed with time, but only festered.

"I would not trade one oppressor for another," the king declared conclusively, resuming his nervous march.

"The Qa will not oppress us, Your Highness," Beggerin replied reassuringly. "Rheged boasts rich soil and bountiful forests. We have no such resources for them to plunder – only deep lakes and steep mountains."

"We have people, do we not?" the king responded, his elocution becoming histrionic, his posture erect. "And are we not the Keepers of the One Land?"

Durdich's national myth harked back to the Second Age – a time before the idea of kings and kingdoms had even been conceived. The

13

Kings of Durdich were revered as incarnates of the first men of Tur, the Keepers of Alba, who would one day see that pan-Turian realm restored. The Rhegish intelligentsia viewed such claims as delusional, heathen, and worst of all treasonous. Durdich was not alone in predicating its legitimacy on primeval legend: the Great Oak of Rheged, the paramount symbol of the Old Kingdom, was boasted to have been planted by the Keepers themselves. Yet the Durdish tradition deliberately subverted this claim: the Silver Birch of Ibar, Durdich's own emblem, represented the death of the Empire of Rheged and the rebirth of the One Land of Alba.

Faith in such a future had waned ever since Drochduil's firstborn son, to whom he had passed his name, one day vanished, never to be seen again. Drochduil's second son, Eogan Rannish, had tried to restore the line by giving his own son the name of Ibar Drochduil; yet on his twelfth birthday, Drochduil the Third disappeared in the same way as the Second. Some said that the sons of Ibar had been cursed with the Madness of the Sea, sailing to their deaths in search of the Lost Land. Others imagined that the they had been taken there by the Keepers, the patriarchs of Alba, to await the day when the One Land was restored.

Rannish's only other child was Bassien Conlaoch. Born out of wedlock, Conlaoch was unable to pass the name of Ibar to his own son, Bassien Dunragit, who was bound to pass the bastard name of Bassien to his offspring and his offspring's offspring, forever through the generations. To spare her the same fate, Conlaoch sent Dunragit's sister Breaca to a nunnery, the House of Ayla, where she would remain celibate until her death. Thus was ended the line of Ibar; and thus was born the prophecy that one day it would it would be restored, along with Alba itself. Like his father, Dunragit had seized this prophecy with zeal. Ever was he tormented by the scourge of his name, a constant proclamation to all of Tur that he would never beget the heir of Ibar. Yet he was a Keeper of Alba; and ever did he desire to be the one who would herald the return of Ibar Drochduil.

"Aye, right you are, Your Highness," Beggerin conceded, having apparently anticipated Dunragit's response, "but is it not the Land which the Empire has desecrated since that accursed battle? And is it not Her people that the Empire has enslaved?"

Dunragit flinched again, this time with the mass of his body. "Reinforce Cromlech," he ordered bluntly after an abrupt turn, "and send a batallion to Glenamara." His second order was faltering, almost inaudible, as if he wished not to countenance its implications.

"Begging your pardon, Your Highness?" Beggerin hissed.

"I said, send reinforcements to the Mara!" the king bellowed. "Make sure those filthy Rhegs don't cross the border!"

Beggerin bowed his hunched back obeisantly in agreement, his permanent smirk becoming slightly more serpentine. "As you command, Your Highness."

~ Chapter 4 ~

Still squinting, the sun had begun to rise from its terrestrial bed. The morning dew was still fresh, and the richness of damp earth still lingered in the autumn air. It would be an hour before the village of Hartsop was awake – before the farmers began to inter seed and exhume crop, before the children congregated to learn and play, before the hawkers commenced their zealous homilies. As was his custom, Mungo Caldbeck was already drawing water from the village well, which lay a stone's throw west of the hamlet amid a copse of yew trees. He would do so leisurely and prayerfully, content in the holiness of his familiar ritual, until the rest of the village arrived to wash, drink, and mingle.

Like many in Brambia, the well was supposedly hewn by the Shai, the race of holymen who had long since vanished from the known world. That was many ages ago, though, and nobody knew for sure why the Priests had journeyed this far from Shailana, or why they had later departed. One account had it that they were travelling merchants; another that they were itinerant evangelists; yet another that they were refugees, fleeing the destruction of their homeland. It was generally agreed that they fled Rheged en masse after the Old Kingdom fell; but that was a dark age in the history of the world, lacking remembrance or record, shrouded in myth and mystery. Mungo would often picture the Priests gathered around the well – which, he imagined, was not so different from the humble trough which now lay before him. Arrayed in pearl-white robes, the ascetic clerics would chant soulfully to Elah as they partook of His life-blood.

Mungo's grandmother had told him countless stories of the Age of Dalriada, when the Shai dwelt among the common folk. Tur was a different world then – one that did not distinguish between magic and mundane, reality and dream, sacred and profane. Indeed, some believed that the Priests were not wholly distinct from the People; rather, all were priests, with miraculous powers of healing and wisdom diffused among young and old, male and female, master and worker. Mungo delighted in the thought of his simple-minded companion Balder Appletree, known mainly for his merry antics in the Crowdundle ale-house, meditating in a hermitage or teaching in the Temple; and indeed, such a world it was.

All that remained of the Priests were scattered traces, such as the unremarkable hole in the ground that served as Mungo's secret sanctuary; and as the world became increasingly preoccupied with power, wealth, and other shadows, their legacy faded further and further into obscurity. Yet Mungo was convinced that the early morning air still carried something of the essence of the Priestly Age, even if he could not explain it or even understand it: it was as if a kind of spirit lingered over the wet ground, ushering in the new day with timeless whispers. Perhaps the backwoods and backwaters of Brambia, overlooked as they were by the venal machinations and vindictive madness of the outside world, had preserved the enchantment of the Ancient Way after all, if only one cared to look for it.

The sun had risen from its tomb by the time Mungo finished his chores; soon it would banish the defeated shadows, which cowered behind makeshift barricades to mount their last, unavailing stand. Enlightened by the heavenly light, inspired by the earthy air, Mungo stood still to observe and absorb the newness of everything.

Mungo was distracted from his meditation when he noticed the portly figure of Beyla Puddingstone, the stepdaughter of Mungo's late uncle, holding up the ends of her oversized frock as she waddled hurriedly towards the well. Beyla, too, held an especial fondness for the well, but for a different reason: it was the perfect place to exchange, incite, and otherwise indulge in gossip. She had barely reached the yew-grove before she cast her bait.

"Are you comin' to the Roundhouse lat'r?" she hollered, referring to the mud-thatched hut where the village convened each week to issue notices and settle disputes. The building stood on the ruins of a more ancient site, and thus, like the well, carried a memory of the Third Age. "Farm'r Musgrave's missin' a flock of sheep, Daisy Clearwat'r's given b'rth to twins, and the first of the gannets an' crakes have been spotted headin' south for the wint'r." Beyla was panting heavily when she finally reached the well, by which time Mungo had already disengaged from the undoubtedly scandalous hearsay. "An' somethin' about that old Rheggish king."

Mungo perked up at the addendum. "You mean Urien of Aelhairn?" he asked with equal eagerness as Beyla's bulletin. "What about him?"

"Well, I don't know, Mungo," Beyla replied teasingly, thrilled that the fish were biting. "I guess you'll have to come along and find out."

Grabbing his water jug and laundry basket, Mungo scurried off into the sunrise.

~ Chapter 5 ~

"Let us start with what we know." Urien and Owein were seated amidst a score of generals, administrators, and military advisors – the War Council of Rheged. The High Commander, a grim-faced, deep-voiced colossus cloaked in the blood-red and molten-gold of Rheged, was initiating proceedings. "The Qa invaded the Helm not from the north, but from the east. They could not have done so unless they had already seized the Durdish garrisons."

"Why, then, did we receive no news that they had fallen?" interjected the corpulent General of Oxenfen, Malvern Brennus. "We were not even aware that they had been attacked. The eastern ridge has been quiet for months!"

"Years," affirmed the stolid Commander. "The Qa have never initiated conflict – they have only ever fought when provoked. As for the Durds, they have committed the bulk of their forces to the Mara, which is a far more vulnerable border." Ever so slightly, the Commander began to trail off from his dispassionate analysis, as if the mention of the River of Blood had scraped against an old wound; but he recovered reflexively, taking the pain in his stride. "Our strategy has long reflected this situation. Our forces were severely outnumbered when the Qa arrived at the Helm."

Owein forced his contribution through clenched teeth. "It seems uncanny, does it not, that the entire eastern range could be captured so expeditiously?" He vaulted to his feet as his restraint collapsed.

"Dunragit has conspired with Dahaka and the rest of the Aramite devils!"

Emrys Morraine, personal advisor to the king, intervened almost before Owein had finished speaking. "Respectfully, Sire," he warbled unctuously, "your personal strife with Bassien Dunragit is understandable – admirable, even – but we know very little at this point. Surely reason dictates that we await the return of our envoy, before making decisions which we may later regret."

"We will not learn anything from the envoy," General Brennus rebutted, "for the Durdish malcontents will tell us nothing of import." The erratic ruffles of his bristly white moustache were accentuated by the laboured puffs of his fiery red face. "Why would they if they have not already?"

Morraine ignored Brennus's question, instead directing his importunity at Owein. "As long as they hold the eastern range, the Qa enjoy a steady supply of reinforcements. It would require the best part of our army to recover the Helm at this stage, let alone to hold it. As the High Commander so helpfully reminded us," Morraine commended fulsomely, as if to jab at an uncovered wound, "those forces are sorely needed at the Mara. The circumstances would be considerably more favourable if Dunragit were to first retake his garrisons."

"And yet for every minute we delay, the task becomes more difficult," the High Commander inserted sedately, unaffected by Morraine's backhanded jibe, "for the Qa are surely fortifying the Helm as we speak."

Urien, who had thus far remained aloof, finally engaged. "We will not reclaim the fortress with the armies of men, with or without the assistance of Dunragit; for this is the fulfilment of the Prophecy of Enoch." The utterance of that hallowed name hushed the council.

"Your Highness, with the utmost respect, we cannot rely on obscure divinations from a bygone age to determine our strategy," Morraine rejoined delicately. "This is a military council, not a temple."

"Indeed it is, Morraine," Brennus seethed, thrusting a plump finger in his antagonist's direction, "which makes your presence all the more bewildering." Morraine launched to his feet at the insult, but was halted when Urien once again spoke up.

"Tell me, Sir Morraine, where are the temples now? Have they not been converted into money-houses? And where are the oracles, the scribes, the rectors? Have they not been disbanded?" With no riposte at hand, Morraine resumed his seat. Urien scanned the faces of his pupils before continuing. "The Prophecy will be recalled nowhere if not here."

"What then would you have us do?" asked Owein, impatient for an answer but restraining his fury. "We cannot just leave the Helm to rot."

Urien gazed piercingly at his son. In a deliberate voice, he replied, "You know what you must do, Your Highness, for you know the Prophecy better than most." Owein averted his eyes, perplexed and embarrassed.

"What are your orders, Sire?" the High Commander eventually rumbled.

Owein, allowing his wrath to subdue his discomfort, delivered his command. "Send a battalion to the Mara. We will force the truth from Dunragit whether he would give it to us or not."

Morraine once again reacted summarily, while the rest of the councillors murmured and muttered. "You would instigate a war with Durdich while our most strategic city lies in Aramean hands? Sire, I beseech you, reconsider this notion."

"On this matter I am obliged to agree with Morraine, Your Highness," the High Commander submitted with a hint of regret. "It seems most ill-advised to multiply our enemies at this critical time."

"And I shall do no such thing," Owein replied sharply. "Once our forces reach the Mara, I will request that they are allowed to secure the Durdish garrisons. This will afford us an additional line of attack on the Helm, provided that Dunragit accedes."

"And if he does not?" Brennus asked gingerly. Even he was unsettled by the imprudence of the plan, which resembled a feud more than a strategy.

"Then we will know that he is an accomplice in this treacherous larceny, and is already our enemy. We will therefore engage him with the full strength of the King's Army."

***

"Your Highness, I must exhort you that this plan will only beget

23

further destruction." Urien and Owein had retired to the royal drawing room, where a crew of parlourmaids served them tea, wine, and liqueurs. Urien continued to plead with Owein, who puffed an outsized chibouk in restless contemplation.

"Please, Father, call me Bedwas – the name that you and Mother gave to me." Owein began to gently gnaw the pipe's copper mouthpiece, as if he were fighting to hold back words.

"As you wish, my son," Urien conceded, his expression remaining purposeful and expectant.

After a few more breaths of smoke, which he watched disperse and disappear, Owein resumed the conversation. "Father, you must tell me why you left, and why you have returned. I will not discuss war, prophecies, or anything else until you have accounted for your untimely absence. It drove Mother mad, and now it is doing the same to me."

Urien gazed out of the adjacent window into the night's bleak, drizzling ether. "I was called, my son," he intoned sombrely, "as you are now."

With that, he began to recount his journey.

~ Chapter 6 ~

Urien was seated study, poring over a cluttered pile of dusty books strewn across his lamplit bureau. Dawn was just beginning to break when his wife appeared in the doorway holding a lantern of her own. "Have you slept at all, Aelhairn?" she murmured groggily.

Urien continued to flip through pages and adjust his eyeglass as he answered her with laboured distraction. "Yes – I mean, some. Earlier."

"Is it the dreams again?" she asked tenderly as she moved behind his chair, gathering his blonde locks into neat bunches.

"Yes, Coira," he replied tersely. Over the course of several years, Urien had developed an acute sense that something was calling him, which he struggled to define. Awaking each morning before sunrise, he would know that he had been visited in his dreams, which he struggled to recall. Studying tales of his predecessors, he would encounter an eerie familiarity, which he struggled to explain. "I am reading about Gwydion Aspatria," he said sleepily, removing his smudgy monocle and scratching his bloodshot eyes, "the Great Father of Dalriada."

Coira shuffled over to a loveseat near the desk. "Is this where you slept?" she asked, concerned yet amused, shoving a heap of linens onto the floor with her spare hand before sitting down.

"Coira, I know where this all began," Urien stated, ignoring her question. "It was in Brambia, a few months before Conlaoch's ambush. I can't remember why I was there, though; nor can I remember why *I*

25

went – why didn't I just send Latrell, or Brennus, or any other officer?"

Coira placed her lamp on an adjacent book-table and leant in towards her husband. "Tell me what you *do* remember, Aelhairn."

Urien furrowed his brow as he delved further into the murky pool of memories. "We were headed for Watendlath, but there was a storm – a terrible storm – so we diverted to the Ghelt. We took shelter in a cave on the banks of the Ashness River and set off the next morning." Urien paused, partially relaxing his crumpled face. "I had a dream that night, Coira. I am unable to recall its substance, but somehow it still haunts me."

"Why have you only now remembered this?" Coira asked.

Suddenly spry, Urien turned to his bulky tome and began to riffle through its timeworn pages. "I was reminded by the story of Gwydion Aspatria," he whispered, as if divulging some unthinkable conspiracy. "He, too, had a vision in the Ghelt – and in a cave, no less!" Eventually he located his desired page. "Look – it's all here," he exclaimed, inverting the volume and thrusting it onto Coira's lap. "Gwydion was Brambian, of course. His native name was Gwydir. He was a merchant who passed into the Ghelt on his way back from Keldas, where he had been trading."

The route described by Urien, over the desolate Mulberry Plains, had long since fallen out of use. After the collapse of trade in the Sixth Age, there was little reason left for anyone to travel between Brambia and the Rheggish centreland – let alone to risk the perils of the Plains, long since used as a hideout for outlaws. The Ghelt, in turn, had

26

become a shadowy wild, its inhabitants migrating to the towns of Brambia or taking their woodcraft to the Bramble, the great forest from which the country took its name.

Yet Urien was nearly certain that the cave described in his book was the very place in which he had himself taken refuge. The annals related that the mouth of the cave was covered by a curtain of water flowing from a perennial spring – and Urien recalled precisely such a curtain covering his own sanctuary, having assumed at the time that it was merely runoff from the torrential downpour. Indeed, he recollected how the mist emanating from the cataract had revealed a miniature rainbow, which he had found especially peculiar given its occurrence during a sunless thunderstorm. Although Urien's manuscript mentioned no such rainbow, it did describe the aqueous veil as "the prism of Heaven".

According to the legends, Gwydir fell into a trance after imbibing from the waterfall, during which he was variously imparted with an ancient wisdom, endowed with a supernatural power, or bestowed with a royal blessing. Urien knew that all of these narratives purported to explain how a humble trader from Brambia succeeded in uniting all of Tur to forge the Ancient Way of Dalriada, heralding a millennium of peace and prosperity. Until now, however, he had dismissed such folklore, along with the entire myth of Dalriada, as mere fantasy.

Coira had listened intently to Urien's monologue. Unlike her sceptical husband, she had always believed in the Prophecy of Enoch, which foretold of a day when the glories of the Old Kingdom and the

Ancient Way would both be restored. "Were there any inscriptions in the cave?" she asked imperatively.

"I know not," Urien abruptly responded, irritated by the digression. "The inside of the cave was pitch dark, for we had no dry wood to start a fire. Why do you ask?"

"It matters not," Coira replied with equal bluntness. "You must leave immediately, Aelhairn, for Elyon is calling you." The utterance of that divine name as it was rendered in the Royal Tongue of Rheged brought Urien's confusion and anxiety to a still silence, for she had expressed that which he knew to be true. "Take with you the companies of Brennus and Latrell," she continued, "for the Plains are more perilous than they were in Gwydion's day."

Urien contemplated his wife's words before taking back the text, once again studying the open page. "No," he concluded. "I must go alone."

~ Chapter 7 ~

Taking his finest mount, Urien reached the town of Oxenfen within a fortnight. Besides his sword, which never left his side, he had carried little more than a blanket, emergency rations, and a few parchments from his study. To conceal his identity, he wore a nondescript cloak with a baggy hood, which flapped wildly as he raced through countless miles of flat grassland, scattered with grazing herds and lonesome homestead. Aided by his manuscripts, which he analysed obsessively at every stopping point, Urien had used the journey to scour his mind for memories, and his memories for meaning.

West of the town, the horizon was dominated by a barren plateau, which extended beyond sight and thought – the Mulberry Plains, thus named both for the purple hue of their metamorphic floor and for the oases of trees that once provided shade and sustenance to weary travellers. Here the King's Road turned northwards, skirting around the formidable massif before terminating at Watendlath, from which the Ghelt could be reached with an additional day's ride.

That was the way he told Coira he would go. From the outset, however, his real intention had been to cut directly across the Plains – once frequented by seasoned traders who conveyed the produce of the Bramble across the continent, but long overrun by marauding brigands who scrapped over meagre spoils. Though Urien was not deterred by the dangers of the Plains, his mount was tiring, and he would need her full vigour to reach Watendlath. Concealing his face in his hood, he found a stable on the outskirts of town and waited for the hostler to retire. The door was locked, but Urien had already planned to enter through the skylight. After dropping onto a pile of hay, he removed the oak beam from a side entrance and led his horse inside. With its sturdy roof and hay-strewn floor, the makeshift inn was surprisingly comfortable. Urien was grateful that he had been forced to rest, though sleep continued to elude him.

He was in full flight across the Plains by daybreak. Riding west, he felt as if the nascent sun was chasing him, earnestly beseeching him not to continue towards the still-dark sky. Even when mid-day finally came, the starkness of the interminable landscape seemed to resist the light, as it if it were eclipsed by some unseen force; and yet it lay fully exposed, like bait in a trap. Once Oxenfen faded from sight, Urien could not rid himself of the feeling that the stone itself was watching him as he moved further and further into its clutches.

Urien rested little that day, pausing only to let his horse gnaw on a patch of scrub or drink from a stagnant puddle. He had hoped to traverse the Plains in a single day, but the unforgiving terrain had delayed him considerably, with the relentless impact of hoof on stone jarring and jading both horse and rider. A vicious gale had also impeded him, as had the indistinctness of the path – though initially a clear thoroughfare, it gradually diminished and eventually disappeared, as if attesting that few who embarked across the Plains ever reached the other side. Estimating that at least three more hours of hard riding would be required to reach the Ghelt, Urien decided that the risk of becoming further disoriented in the darkening dusk outweighed any benefits of persevering. He alighted behind a heap of stones to wait out the night.

Respite from the biting gusts and chafing saddle provided instant relief. Yet Urien had barely settled when, for the first time since beginning across the Plains, he became aware of another rider, prowling surreptitiously across the pavement. He could not be certain, though, that he was not merely reliving the repetitive motion of the day's ride, for the the distant resonance barely penetrated the howling wind, and the evanescent sunlight had nearly dissipated into the endless expanse. As he strained his senses to verify the suspicion, he heard the same recurrent clump, this time coming from the opposite direction, this time close and unmistakeable. He was being ambushed.

Adrenaline impelled both man and beast, their raucous retreat precluding any attempt to see or hear their predators. As the horse fatigued, however, Urien was able to discern a handful of highwaymen, whose malevolent intentions were confirmed by an arrow that whistled past his ear. Amid the peril, Urien thought of his beloved son, whom he had left without farewell and without a father. After stamping his heels into the sides of his exhausted carrier without effect, he drew his sword and pricked the creature's hide to elicit one final, desperate surge that brought him within sight of his objective – the forgotten forest of the Ghelt, which appeared to him like land to a soul lost at sea.

It was not long, however, before his horse was pierced again, this time by an assailant's arrow, causing it to stagger and eventually stumble to the ground. Sheathing his sword, Urien continued the race on foot, expecting at any moment to suffer the same fate; but the icy pang of sharp steel never came. Glancing back, he could see that the bandits had halted in their tracks. Looking forward, he identified the unexpected and unexplainable source of their deterrence: a lone figure, stooped over a cane, waiting resolutely on the edge of the woods as if to guard his domain, as if the vast multitude of trees was his army. After swivelling his head in disbelief to verify that his hunters had relented, Urien squinted his eyes to examine the sentinel, who duly withdrew into the pitch-black forest.

His heart pounding and his lungs heaving, Urien paused at the threshold of the wood before reluctantly entering the murky realm. A thick cocoon of dank, mossy air immediately enveloped him, providing a welcome if oppressive contrast to the naked exposure of the Plains. With visibility extinguished, however, he could not proceed far before becoming entangled in a prickly jumble of briers and nettles. As he struggled to free himself, he lost his footing and fell backwards. His head hit something hard and his consciousness submitted to the darkness of the forest.

~ Chapter 8 ~

Urien awoke with a wrenching ache pulsating through his skull. He tried to sit up, but found that he was ensnared in a vast web of undergrowth and overgrowth, which twisted and weaved from beneath the ground to the tops of the trees. The tortuous thicket seemed to have enveloped him during his coma, to have absorbed him into its organism. Either he had been unconscious for a lifetime, or the plant-life had grown miraculously; but either way, the place seemed to be free from the passage of time, as if Elyon had kept it apart when He set the world in motion. The forest seemed to exist unchangingly in some primordial, transcendent age; yet, at the same time, it seemed to be always growing, as if to counterbalance the world's decay.

Urien reached for his sword. He managed to cut himself free from the snare, but the battle was hard won; and as he headed further into the jungle, he found every step to be just as arduous, with the sodden morass and the stifling humidity further hindering his advance. With his provisions abandoned on the Mulberry Plains, Urien had no means of sustaining such an effort, and was eventually compelled to seek nourishment. The forest, however, only mocked him with stagnant pools and strange fungi, which he eschewed despite his parched throat and cramping stomach. As he hobbled on, the swipes of his sword became increasingly impotent.

Urien was on the brink of surrender when he heard a twig snap. Reflexively, he crouched low and clasped his sword. Now that he had stopped, he could hear a rhythmic rustle of leaves and brush – footsteps. At first, he could perceive nothing through the jumble of the jungle; but eventually he caught sight of the warden of the wood, wilted with wrinkles and coated in rags, making his way through the intricate matrix with inexplicable ease, as if his gnarled staff were a sceptre to which nature itself would bow. Should he call out to this stranger, who had intimidated a horde of criminals? What kind of person would live in such a place, and why? Given the ruckus caused by his trespass, Urien surmised that his counterpart must have become aware of his presence long ago; yet the gaunt, hoary woodsman continued to glide through the bush, unperturbed if not oblivious, until he was once again out of sight.

Urien sidled furtively through the foliage to reach the path fashioned by the wayfaring hermit. The mustiness of the forest seemed to vanish in this royal highway as a light breeze awakened the air, caressing Urien's golden locks in a way that reminded him of Coira. There was no seduction, though; for a strangely familiar benevolence assured Urien that this was the Yom of Kippur, the very Song of Elyon – a song of marriage, of forgiveness, of reconciliation. Urien yielded to its timeless lyrics, allowing its life-giving voice to carry him forward, through, and beyond.

Urien sailed through the passage for hours, with no impression of weight or will, until he was roused by the quiet sound of flowing water. He realised that he had been following the river for some time, but so mellifluous was its tune, so restful its rhythm, that his tired mind had simply let it be. Indeed, it seemed that the water was repeating the speech of the wind in a seamless litany, or playing the same tune on a different instrument. Although the river remained out of sight, Urien could see that his path soon widened into a broad clearing – a green, open pasture, where the flickering shadows of the forest vanished under a chandelier of untainted sunlight.

The sound of the river was louder here, but Urien was immediately preoccupied by another noise, that of a frenzied rustle in the surrounding brushwood. Scanning the perimeter, he spotted a speckled doe caught in the thicket. His instinct was to reach for an arrow and ready his bow, but, those implements absent, he resorted instead to his trusty blade. The deer, at first convulsing with terror, froze as Urien approached. The two creatures locked eyes, as if pleading with each other, until the prey finally yielded to its fate. There was no struggle when the slaughter finally came, only flinches of pain and gasps of desperation; but there was blood aplenty, and Urien was left standing in a crimson pool by the time the deed was done.

Butchering the animal was easier than hacking through the forest, but it took longer than usual to kindle a fire owing to the dampness of the wood. Once ignited, it emitted a thick smoke which only thickened as he offered up his sacrifice, rising steadily above the treetops and to the heavens. Urien watched and waited as the meat crackled and sizzled on the end of his spit. After devouring what he could, he lay down on the soft grass and let the flame die out, at which point he cast his idle gaze to the evening sky. His eyelids gradually drooped as the sun dropped below the canopy.

When he awoke a half-day later, his first sensation was the metallic bitterness of dried plasma which coated his tongue and encrusted his mouth. His urgent thirst reminded him of the river, close at hand, and somewhere on its banks the elixir of Gwydion Aspatria. After climbing to his feet, he began to search the boundaries of the clearing for a path towards the water. He was half-way around the field when he espied the itinerant woodsman, standing motionless on the opposite side, just as he had when Urien first saw him from the Mulberry Plains. The two creatures held each other's gaze, each waiting for the other to act. Although the character was some way off, Urien could see into his eyes; and in them he saw unmistakably the same wildness, and the same gentleness, which he had seen in the eyes of his former prey. The elder finally retreated into the woods, which duly yielded to their advancing master.

When sight and sound were clear, Urien inched cautiously across the field. He was certain this was the side from which he had entered the evening prior; but when he peered into the path taken by the elusive phantom he found not the expansive road he expected, but rather a narrow, winding trail, barely distinct from the surrounding vegetation. He proceeded warily, clutching his blood-stained sword, only to be welcomed by a familiar breeze which now flowed away from the clearing. Urien relaxed into its soothing recital of sacred psalms, which crescendoed into a soulful chorus: the Ashness River, resounding with praise and thanksgiving. Urien dashed to its sandy banks. After lapping up its sweet, clear water, he threw off his sullied clothes and baptised his body in its cool, blessed depths.

He was floating on his back, once again gazing into the firmament, when his eye caught a glimmer of light flickering halfway up the red sandstone cliffs which towered over the opposite shoreline. At first, the lustre of the reflection prevented him from ascertaining its source, but after a few sideways paddles he could identify a small waterfall pouring over the aperture of a dark hollow. Urien began swimming excitedly to what he could only imagine to be Gwydir's cave. It was not long, though, before the question entered his mind: how does it lie on the other side of the river? Urien never crossed the Ashness when he first happened on the cave, and neither did he expect to do so this time. His pace slowed as his reasoning accelerated. Perhaps the approach from the Mulberry Plains was divergent to that from the King's Road due a meander in the river. After all, he thought to himself, the Ghelt remains uncharted, excepting a few primitive sketches. Perhaps, he dared to imagine, Gwydion himself had crossed the river at this very spot.

Engrossed in a frenzy of deliberation, he had already mounted the riverbank when he remembered his nakedness. He considered retrieving his clothes, but, with his prize within reach, he could not bear to delay. Instead, he began searching impatiently for a way to ascend the sheer bluff that confronted him, finally locating a scree-filled gully that tapered up the precipice. The barefoot climb was nearly impossible: for every step that he gained, the splintered scree would collapse yet further, leaving his feet injured and his position unimproved. With his extremities bleeding and bruised, Urien eventually arrived at the bottom of a narrow shelf indented into the aspect of the rock. After side-stepping across the rubble, he hoisted himself up to the ledge to find himself on a path, staring at a forgotten yet familiar sight. His company had reached this very path from the top of the bluff, hoping it led to the river. Instead, it led to Gwydion's cave.

Urien's eagerness to reach the cave was checked by a haunting premonition. Exactly what happened in the Ghelt had eluded his recollection ever since he read his own past in the legend of Gwydion Aspatria; but now, here he was, reliving his fate. Indeed, as he shuffled along the shelf, time and space seemed to orbit each other, forming ever-new constellations of existence but never coalescing into here and now. Was he recalling dormant memories, or was this yet another dream, which he would forget upon awakening? There was little difference in this enchanted dimension, which seemed more real than reality itself despite existing in the universe of imagination.

Though the song of flowing water had been present throughout Urien's traverse, a quieter rendition, distinguished by the calm, continuous collision of water and rock, informed him that the waterfall was close at hand. When he rounded the final bend, it seemed that the cave was waiting for him: it seemed to dwell in the fullness of the present, as if proclaiming, with every drop of water which flowed never-endingly over its face, that eternity was now. The kaleidoscope of colours that refracted from the waterfall appeared to shine forth from everlasting to everlasting, marking the point at which Heaven had given birth to earth, and earth to Heaven.

At this point in his quest, Urien had expected ravishment, rhapsody, rapture. Somehow, though, as he approached his journey's end, he perceived that he was in fact arriving at its beginning. It was as if he was to be reborn as one who had always existed, but must first undergo the death of that which must no longer exist. The cave was at once a tomb of the old and a womb of the new.

Urien paused at the threshold of the sanctuary. The veil over the cave's mouth mirrored the veil over his mind's eye, which fluttered tantalisingly to reveal dim reflections of the world beyond. That world beckoned him with a promise of salvation; yet the world behind bound him with an assurance of control, for he knew that there was no chance of reneging once the covenant had been ratified. An incipient wind enlivened his naked body, which was swaddled in a blanket of chilled sweat, and animated the primordial forest, which broke out in a rousing chorus of applause. It was the Yom of Katzir, Elyon's Laughter, said to be contained in the first cry of every newborn child.

Finally, Urien stepped through the translucent doorway. The clear, colourful water poured over his head and spilled down his body, anointing him as he passed from the profane to the consecrated, from the superficial intimations of the seen and the known to the secret intimacy of the world within. His knees trembled as he felt his mind being exposed, like one who had long lived in darkness encountering a great, unfathomable light.

As he staggered forward, his attention was swiftly drawn to a collage of inscriptions which covered the interior of cave. Thanks to his royal schooling, Urien immediately recognised the script as Tura – the lost language of the Keepers of Alba. He ran his finger over the intricate engravings, preserved despite the ages. He yearned to comprehend the holy text, which he fancied to have been hewn by Gwydir himself; or perhaps, he imagined, it had been there since the very foundation of the world.

As he surveyed the composition, which seemed to listen as much as it told, Urien detected a faint wisp of smoke. He turned to locate its source – a rudimentary hearth at the back of the cave, emitting the last traces of a dying fire. On his last visit, it was apparent that the place had been occupied shortly before his arrival, and the same was true this time. As Urien toured the rest of the den, each of his footsteps reverberated several times before fading into the unbroken resonance of the eternal spring. The waterfall – that was why he was here.

Urien ran his hand under the organic fountain. The temperature of the water was like liquid ice, its consistency like liquid glass. The waterfall eclipsed the world outside, which somehow appeared more, not less vivid, as if the cataract was a lens, revealing the latent force that enlivens all life. He cupped his hands and lent forward into the falling water, as if commencing a prayer. As he peered into his feeble chalice, which constantly leaked but was constantly filled, he realised that this was the culmination of his quest, of his dreams, and indeed, of his very life. With relief and anticipation, he raised his palms to his mouth, and drank.

***

Owein had abandoned his pipe some while ago, having become enthralled with Urien's narrative to the point of ignoring the maidservant's overture of additional refreshments. The daylight had all but expired; a collection of lanterns imbued the room with a dim glow. Owein could not tell whether his father had finished or merely paused his recountal.

Owein's scepticism was inherited from his father. He used to enjoy hearing his mother recount the tales of the Old Fathers of Rheged – his own ancestors, whom, in the popular imagination, the Shai had bestowed with the Cornerstone of Shailoh to continue the Ancient Way of Dalriada. He could still recite the Prophecy of Enoch, which his mother Coira had transposed into a melodious rhyme that he still found himself humming while he strolled through the royal gardens. As his father's son, however, he had come to accept the stories as romantic allegories rather than authentic histories. To hear Urien speak with such conviction on the same subject that he had once disparaged was jarring. Owein could not suppress his discomfiture. "But where you have been all this time, father? Surely your journey through the Ghelt could not have spanned forty years!"

"That is a story for another time, Bedwas," Urien responded with fatherly compassion, "for it is a story of another world. Now you must sleep, for tomorrow will require your full strength."

Although his mind was racing, Owein was weary of questions; every time he sought to answer one, a dozen more would emerge. Did his father fancy that he had acquired clairvoyant abilities during his unseasonable absence, or was he simply expressing a calculated prediction? It did not bear contemplation. Standing to his feet, he wished his father a perfunctory "Goodnight" before marching to his bedchamber.

~ Chapter 9 ~

Nobody knew if there was a world beyond the shores of Tur; if there was, it had long been lost. Since the Dark Ages, scores of explorers, fugitives, and paupers had sailed in all directions of the compass, only to be swallowed by the horizon. A few neighbouring islets remained inhabited, and primitive ships still skirted parts of the continent; but as the Kingdom of Rheged had declined, travel and trade had dwindled. Much of the ocean was in any case unnavigable: the wind was either too fierce or too calm, and the coastline was beset by shoals, reefs, and other treacherous fouls.

In some quarters, it was believed that the waters were cursed by the Shai, either to shield their retreat from genocide, to avenge their expulsion into exile, or to prevent the rampant depravity of Tur from spreading beyond its shores. Even those who dismissed the story were inclined to recount it, if only to deter their children from harboring fantasies of intrepid exploration. Less commonly remembered was the promise of restoration, bequeathed by the departing Priests and preserved in the names of the Twelve Seas, corresponding to the Twelve Pillars of Shailoh: Emerald, Jasper, Beryl, Sapphire, Ruby, Amethyst, Onyx, Agate, Olivine, Topaz, Turquoise, and Jacinth.

For those who dreamed of the fulfilment of the Promise, the legend of Iona provided a glimmer of hope. Little was known about Gildas Bedwyr, the fabled saint commonly associated with this mythical island. Following a vision, Gildas was said to have embarked from the abandoned port of Lanercost in a primitive coracle, surrendering his passage to the will of Elyon. Like the fleeing Priests, he was sheltered from the savage seas, and after three days of drifting came ashore on an uncharted island. In one version of the story, Gildas discovered a small community of exiled Priests, who had been appointed to remain in hiding until the Shai returned en masse; in another, he established his own community, composed of disciples from across Tur who experienced the same vision and set out in faith across the raging waters. In all of its forms, however, the story of Iona had fallen into myth, even among those who were fond of retelling it – the world was too bleak, too cruel, too real for it to be anything more than a flight of fancy, a whimsical means of escape contrived by the desperate and the faint-hearted.

A less romantic story of migration was found in the Qa people, who were thought to have arrived on the continent of Tur in the same age. The Qa were an altogether distinct race, with an appearance, tongue, and culture that bore no resemblance to the rest of the civilised world. According to their oral histories – for they possessed no manner of written language – they originated from the Islands of Qahal, the Land of the Heart, whose existence seemed indisputable but whose location remained a mystery. Echoing the myth of the cursed seas, the Qa believed that their homeland was engulfed by a vengeful sea-god, forcing their ancestors to set sail in search of asylum. Eventually the refugees washed up on the rock-ribbed coast of Aram, a region beyond the Abaddon Mountains rich in iron ore but almost too inhospitable for human habitation.

There was evidence that the Qa were once scattered across the continent, living among its people; but, through coercion or volition, they were confined to the land of Aram at some point in the distant past. The Qa remained in this desolate corner of Tur for at least an age with no intention of meddling with the affairs of their accidental neighbours until Gorsedd Cadell brought his invidious vision of empire to bear. Cadell's barbaric crusades into the hinterlands of Tur found staunch support in a people embittered by the decline of the Old Kingdom and intoxicated by the notion of a victorious Rheged, rising from ashes to restore the glories of its past. Cadell's avarice, however, only precipitated Rheged's collapse, ushering in the long Age of Darkness. Sharing a common bulwark in the Mountains of Abaddon, Aram and Durdich had forged an alliance of convenience to repel their colonial rulers, whose reckless warmongering had left their own country without the means to sustain further conquest. Rheged eventually abandoned its frontiers, withdrawing its forces even from those regions that were subdued, including the dense forests of Brambia in the West, the bucolic prairies of Farstead in the South, and the peat hags of the Hawes in the North. In the East, however, the violence of Gorsedd Cadell was not easily forgotten.

***

Dunragit had scarcely left his throne room for three days as he monitored the unfolding crisis – a crisis which he had unwittingly created. Each hour he would request the latest news from Cromlech, the unassailable fortress which guarded the ashen badlands of

Abaddon. Along with Lahai to the north and the Helm to the west, the deterrence of Cromlech secured a tenuous peace between the three kingdoms – a peace which had been increasingly eroded by mutual suspicions and veiled threats.

Dunragit's real interest, however, lay not in the godforsaken mountains of Abaddon, but in the bloodstained valley of the Mara. The thunderous river which bisected that narrow ravine wailed unremittingly for the countless atrocities it had witnessed, brutally scouring its disfigured banks in a vain attempt to cleanse its defilement. The twin cities of Glaramara and Glenamara stood defiantly on either side, teeming with vindictive bitterness, consumed by ancient grievances. If Brackentrod represented the height of enmity between Durd and Rheg, the Mara represented its depth – for it was there that Cadell's hatred had taken root most deeply, and it was there that retribution had been most fierce.

Dunragit had summoned the war council as soon as he received word from the Rhegish frontier. He now waited restlessly at the Round Table, a single cross-section of a giant maple trunk situated below a concentric balcony. Cadell had administered the construction of this amphitheatrical court as a display of Durdich's subservience: the indigenous government would convene on the ground level, overseen by a regime of Rhegish proconsuls. After he established the sovereign Land of Durdich, Ibar Drochduil ordered that the mezzanine gallery be preserved as a permanent reminder of Rheged's tyranny. Since then, however, its crimson-gold banners had accumulated a thick layer of dust which appropriately resembled the indigo-silver theme of the newfound realm.

"We will conduct the meeting ourselves if the council does not appear momentarily." Dunragit was speaking to Vicereine Maran Osla, the only woman on the Council and the only other member to have arrived. Like the proconsul's balcony, the colonial system of ranks and titles had persisted in an incidental fashion. Officially, Osla was commissioned by the king to superintend the affairs of the provincial administration. Since the latter had assumed the status of national government, it was of little consequence that the system originated as an instrument of foreign rule. On the contrary, Durdish officials revelled in the irony of adapting the title of Viceroy to Maran Osla when Cadell had explicitly banned the admission of females into the state apparatus.

"With reverence, Your Highness," Osla commented calmly, "you dispatched the council to Cromlech not one week ago to negotiate with the Qa. I expect that they have not yet returned."

"I recalled them three days ago," Dunragit responded tetchily. "They were due back this morning." On cue, a band of short-winded, bedraggled functionaries came bumbling into the room, leaving a trail of mud and odour. Dunragit seemed not to notice their disheveled state. "At last!" he exclaimed, without so much as a salutation. "Sit, all of you," he ordered, flicking his hand across the table and rustling through a pile of documents. As the ragtag bevy fumbled into their chairs, a final pair entered the chamber. One of them hobbled cumbrously, his back stooped over a cane, while the other sauntered leisurely alongside to maintain a hushed conversation. Dunragit took especial notice of the unlikely duo. "Beggerin," he declared, identifying the ungainly hunchback, "I did not expect you to return in time." After a stern abeyance, he turned to the accomplice. "And Morraine – I had not expected you at all."

"There is news from Rheged, Your Highness," Begerrin deflected as he struggled into his chair. "It has been reported that Aelhairn Urien has returned from his sequestration." Beggerin began to enunciate his words more carefully, as if anticipating their impact. "And that he intends to restore the Old Kingdom."

Urien's infamy in Durdich was second only to that of Cadell, for he was known as the murderer of Bassien Conlaoch, Dunragit's father and Drochduil's grandson. The fact that Urien had been acting to defend his retinue against a trap set by Conlaoch himself had been replaced by a slanderous distortion, made all the more potent by its evocative setting. The windswept isle of Tiree off the southern coast of Durdich had been permanently seared into the collective viscera after Cadell's armies incinerated both its land and its people in a blaze so colossal that it could be seen from Cromlech at midday. The charred remains served as a poignant memorial for those who would mourn the dead – and a rousing emblem for those who would avenge them.

The truth was that Urien had more reason than any to curse the name of Cadell; for his own grandfather, Aelhairn Uther, had been knifed in his sleep by a traitorous general who had conspired with

Cadell to seize the throne. Urien's father, Aelhairn Eirnin, had reclaimed the kingdom in an act of valour worthy of an Old Father; and in an act of mercy worthy of a Priest, Urien had himself endeavoured to atone for Cadell's malice – to not only acknowledge Durdich as a sovereign realm, but to help rebuild it. Yet the One Land's resentment could not be allayed. Urien's idealism served only to invite betrayal from Conlaoch, whose illegitimate parentage spurred him to seek his people's affection. Although Owein and Dunragit had agreed a provisional armistice, their familial vendettas continued to rankle. Lasting peace, let alone true reconciliation, seemed more distant than ever.

Dunragit dropped into his chair at the mention of his father's adversary. "Reported? By whom?" When Beggerin failed to provide an immediate answer, the king began gyrating his neck so as to thrust his gaze into everyone's eyes at once.

After clearing his throat, Emrys Morraine responded decorously. "It was I, Your Highness."

Before Morraine could elaborate, Dunragit's impatience erupted. "Well, speak, man!" he commanded as his fist struck the Table with resounding force.

"I beheld him with my own eyes, Your Highness. I shared a council with him – much like this one, only comprised of less honourable persons and governed by a less sagacious king." Morraine cleared his throat again. "He is advising Owein on his war strategy."

"This means nothing, Sire," opined Berlewen Hoel, Master of the

Dowager Guild. Unlike their Rhegish equivalents, the generals of Durdich were not designated specific areas of land, since the land itself was deemed sovereign – though it made little difference in practice, since the land could not wage war or demand tribute. "Since Urien's disappearance the captains of Rheged have grown grey-haired, its armies old-fashioned. Owein has failed to improve his forces for decades – Urien's return will not change that."

Dunragit ignored Hoel, instead directing his query at Morraine. "What is the nature of his strategy?"

Morraine responded carefully. "All I know, Your Highness, is that they sent a full battalion to the Mara some ten days ago, the evening before I departed."

Osla lent forward to attract the king's attention. "Sire, Rhegish troops were seen arriving in Glaramara last night," she confirmed.

Dunragit's eyes ignited, his wild anxiety morphing into focused wrath. "Have our defences in the Glen been fortified to full capacity?"

"Yes, Sire, in accordance with your directive on the Third Moon of Autumn," Osla replied. "General Uchdryd commands the division."

The king's command was decisive. "Tell him to prepare for battle."

~ Chapter 10 ~

The hubbub of the souk was in full swing. The throng of bustling bodies, the clutter of jumbled objects, the babble of spirited voices, the melange of mingling odours – from this primordial chaos sprang the order of life. Merchants hawked and haggled, old friends loafed and loitered, children waged war and kept score in their worlds of make believe. Frugal and carefree, the people of Pashador gathered here each day to exchange goods, jokes, and arguments.

The poverty of the city's inhabitants was contradicted by an imposing semblance of grandeur. Proud edifices of masterfully chiselled slate watched over the multitudes as they performed their duties, shielding them from the distractions of the horizon – to the southwest, the lingering spectre of the Abaddon Mountains; to the northeast, the naked mystery of the Onyx Sea. In the halcyon days of the Old Kingdom, the exquisite masonry of the Qa was famous across Tur, with the finest weapons on the continent hewn from the mines of Dalgada and wrought in the guilds of Pashador, Sychar, and other centres of commerce and craftsmanship. Aramean artefacts were still used as showpieces and heirlooms among the moneyed classes of Durdich and Rheged; but Cadell's crusades had occluded the trade routes of old, leaving the Qa to eke their livelihood from hard rock and wild sea. Some had resorted to piracy and racketeering to subsist, while others had become slaves or slave-traders. Most, however, had simply endured.

Few indigenous Turs had ever entered the land of Aram, and even fewer had ventured beyond Lahai, the bleak redoubt erected by the Qa to match the strongholds of Cromlech and the Helm. It was there that any diplomatic negotiations were held, for no Tur wished to navigate the vast intertidal basin that formed the bulk of the country; nor did any Qa wish for them to do so. To the rest of the continent, Aram remained unknown, alien, other – an object of fear, blame, and hatred. In the popular psyche, the revered sage had been replaced by a dangerous sorcerer, the trustworthy merchant by a devious villain, the skilful artisan by a vulgar brute.

Each Qa family adopted the name of its eldest living male, in relation to whom every other member was identified. Thus, Dahaka Ram, known outside of Aram simply as Dahaka, was in fact son of the father to whom the namesake belonged. Neither Dahaka nor Dahaka Ram was king of the Qa, for the Qa had no king. Indeed, they had no formal system of rule that would be recognisable to a Rheg or a Durd – a peculiarity which only facilitated their vilification. Upon alighting the rocky shores of Aram, however, the Qa were compelled to nominate a figurehead, a spokesperson who would represent their race in the arenas of power. Dahaka's ancestor had evidently been chosen to bear this responsibility, which Dahaka Ram had prematurely assumed after his father contracted the waterborne plague that bedevilled the country. Countless others had already succumbed to the deadly pestilence, which bred in the tidal pools that remained stagnant until Hanavi, the Time of High Water, arrived each year to cleanse the land.

Dahaka Ram was strolling through Pashador's daily fish market, accompanied by his friend and cousin, Hruden Raman, son of Hruden Ram, son of Hruden.

"Morraine cannot be trusted," Hruden Raman insisted as his companion stopped to examine a crate of molluscs. "Neither can Beggerin. Their promise of peace with Durdich smells of deception."

Dahaka had picked up a clam from the create. He sniffed it and theatrically feigned disgust. "Are you sure it isn't the clams?" he joked. Suddenly humourless, he added, "each week the harvest is less fresh." He gazed at the hardy creature, rubbing its mottled shell with his calloused thumb. It had shielded itself tenaciously from the perils of the sea, possibly for hundreds of years, carving out a dismal existence for itself in the dregs of the earth – only to be disinterred, disgraced, and eventually devoured by a predator from another world. It may have even produced a pearl, a gem of great value which some lord or lady would wear on their person as if to claim its beauty; but still the creature would be treated with contempt. He tossed it back into the pile and continued walking.

Hruden continued to press his case, sidestepping the sundry obstacles of the souk to keep abreast with Dahaka. "Morraine is playing the kingdoms off against each other. His initial plan was ingenious, but flawed: it relied on Owein being reasonable enough not to face two enemies at once. That role he reserved for us; and yet it was our own ingenuity that foiled his plot." Hruden stepped across Dahaka to dodge an oncoming cart. "Having failed to prevent war between the Turs, he now bids to profit from their mutual destruction. And Beggerin – that devil would see the world burn if he could rule over its ashes."

Dahaka stopped again, this time next to a fishmonger broiling a haul of grey mullets over an open firepit. "Of course you are right, my friend", he admitted, watching the drama of the flame unfold before him, "but Tur will burn one way or another." Hruden's agitation morphed into astonishment, but Dahaka was soldered to the scene. "Indeed, it is already burning. There is hatred on this continent that will only be quenched by fire."

~ Chapter 11 ~

The Mara waited helplessly as her sorrows, nightmares, and premonitions closed in around her. She laboured with all her substance to separate her children, to save them from each other's hatred; but the depths of destruction into which their forefathers had plunged only yawned wider. She was the verge on which the battle was poised, the abyss into which the dead would descend, the cistern from which this bloodthirsty generation would drink its fill.

Troops had been flowing into the twin cities for nearly a week, every manoeuvre prompting counter-manoeuvre until the entire conurbation formed an intricate web of potential cause and uncertain effect, a stack of dry tinder awaiting a spark.

Emrys Morraine was all too willing to provide it.

***

Malvern Brennus came bumbling into the room, his corrugated face sweating profusely, his stout frame heaving for air.

"Sire, conflict has broken out at the Mara. Glara sustained heavy attack from the enemy's archers three nights ago and the battle has been raging since." Owein sprung up from his throne as Brennus delivered the news. "Nine dead, twenty-odd wounded last we heard. So far it's just volleys – no troops have crossed the river from either side."

Reflexively, Owein began barking a continuous stream of orders and expletives, his strained face quickly engorging with blood as he neglected to replenish his lungs. Before long, the Council had been mustered.

"Where in the Twelve Seas is Morraine, that duplicitous weasel?" Owein bellowed to the assemblage. "And where is Aelhairn?" His voice was more restrained, as if he were addressing the question to himself.

The High Commander replied with unfazed frankness. "Morraine left Wetherstag nearly a fortnight ago, Your Highness. He is reported to be visiting an ailing relative in Tabor." Owein growled under his breath before the Commander turned more hesitantly to the second query. "King Urien has not been seen since this morning. His location remains unknown."

Cullen Latrell, General of Oban, leaned forward from his position near the end of the table. "One of the palace guards registered an irregular incident in the Third Hour involving King Urien, Your Highness," he added circumspectly.

"What incident? What happened?" Owein was at the end of his tether with his father's irregularities.

"I know not, Sire," Latrell replied. "One of my aides handled the record."

***

"I was at my post in the Garden of Shemesh," the guard recounted diffidently. "King Urien was there, visiting the grave of Her Majesty Aelhairn Coira under the Great Oak." That tremendous tree ascended high above the royal cemetery in which its roots were buried, its branches providing shade for generations of resting souls. "He was kneeling – I think he was crying…" The narrator trailed off, embarrassed to be depicting the king in such an intimate situation.

"Well, go on," Brennus ordered brusquely. Owein remained silent, knowing that his voice would expose his emotions; the thought of his mother and father being reunited in such a way after forty years was too poignant for him to subdue.

"When he stood to leave – well, there was a breeze, you see…" The guard was stumbling over his words, apparently bewildered by what he had witnessed.

"Spit it out, man!" Brennus barked, as if threatening to seize what he demanded by force.

"When the tree moved in the wind, the sun shone through the branches into my eyes and I couldn't see," the guard responded, having decided to establish the facts before grappling with their explanation. There was a sustained silence before the account resumed, but this time nobody interjected. "When I could see again, he was gone."

"What do you mean, 'he was gone'?" Owein demanded peevishly, his frustration now outweighing his sentimentality. "Where did he go?"

"I don't know, Sire," the guard replied. Wonderstruck, he lifted his eyes from the ground, to the sky, and back again, as if concluding that the answer lay in both. "He was just…gone."

~ Chapter 12 ~

When Urien awoke, he was standing upright, facing one of the spherical grotto's infinite corners. He had dreamt a dream more vivid than wakefulness, revealing what no eye has seen, what no ear has heard, what no mind has ever conceived. The elusive vagabond had appeared, but transformed: his tattered rags into majestic robes, his knotty cane into an elegant staff, his wrinkled face into a radiant star. Somehow, this metamorphosis had seemed appropriate, as if it was unveiling the subject's true form.

Since he left Wetherstag, Urien had felt as if he were living in one of his dreams, as if he were the protagonist in a story that he was himself telling. Yet something had changed since he drank from Gwydir's spring. As he dwelt in the heart of the earth, he somehow felt fully alive, as if the stone of his own heart had been made flesh. It was as if his dream had become reality, as if his story had merged into the present.

Once his eyes had adjusted, he looked again to the graven runes, strewn across the sandstone dome like a wild vine, hanging before him as if offering him its forbidden fruit. The words seemed to have ripened since he fell asleep; they appeared less obscure, less alien. As Urien inspected the inscriptions, Gwydir's name surfaced unexpectedly in his mind. He scanned the text to identify the source of the impression: *Gwyr,* the Shai name for the venerated saint, transcribed unmistakeably on the wall in front of him.

Incredulously, Urien realised that he was now able to decipher the archaic text. He started with the encompassing sentence: *In the Third Age of Tur, Gwyr Avram here established the Way of Dalriada.* Before proceeding, he glanced around the cave to confirm that he was not still dreaming. A fire had been kindled in the hearth, next to which lay the clothes that he had discarded on the far side of the river, now washed, dried, and neatly folded. Propped against the wall was Trusmadoor, his trusty sword, twinkling regally in the incandescent flame. Doubting his own consciousness but lacking an alternative, he turned again to study the scripture.

~ Chapter 13 ~

"Did Keir not submit our proposal to the Durds? Is that not why we sent him?" Owein was hurrying back towards the palace, trying to maintain a semblance of order while his mind oscillated between the dual crises of his father and the war. His generals were struggling to match his pace.

Brennus shouldered the open question. "If so, it was evidently not received in good will," he wheezed. "Uchdryd would not have taken kindly to the notion of our troops marching on Durdish garrisons, whether or not the troops were accompanied by his own, and whether or not the garrisons were occupied by the Qa."

Owein swivelled to face his retinue, his appearance drained and drawn. "I did not expect him to. He is a zealot. But the proposal should have been referred to Mallerstang, in which case we should not have received a response for another week." Owein turned back and dropped his voice, as if speaking to himself. "It was intended as a message for Dunragit – to inform him that I am alert to his trickery and that he may as well show his hand."

"Liadan Keir," Latrell sneered, shaking his head with contempt. "The imbecile must have panicked, or else offended the Durds with some tactless jibe. Perhaps they misinterpreted his mongrel accent – I can barely understand him most of the time. Remind me – where did we scrape him up from? Some Rhoddian gutter-town, wasn't it?

"Silence!" Owein snapped, again pivoting around but this time flushed and flustered. "Dunragit has matched our forces at the Mara. We must send reinforcements immediately. The city must hold."

"There are no forces to spare, Sire," Latrell pleaded. "We pulled General Keir's battalion from the Turquoise coast. We are already stretched too thinly."

Owein delayed his response, deliberating with himself whether or not to air his thoughts. When he spoke, he did so gravely, as if he would rather not speak at all. "What of Albion?"

It was as if he had violated some sacred taboo. The councillors lowered their eyes, offended and embarrassed, hoping that something or someone would obviate the notion. Owein, though, waited determinedly.

The Wardens of the March had subdued the Marana borderlands with hot-blooded war and cold-blooded rule since the disunion of the kingdoms. Sanctioned to enforce martial law, they soon became warlords who gave no mercy on the battlefield or in the courthouse, mavericks governed only by their ancestral feud. Andras Albion and Iolo Uchdryd had grasped this heritage with fervour; and ever since Urien withdrew Albion from Glaramara as a gesture of peace, they had spoiled for the chance to resume their rivalry.

At last, Latrell spoke up. "Andras Albion cannot be contained, Your Highness, let alone directed – otherwise we would have him overseeing Glara already. His personal strife with Uchdryd risks inducing conflict."

"'*Risks?*'" Owein aped quizzically. "War is upon us, man! Albion commands an entire battalion which currently sits idle. I do not need to direct him – only to unleash him."

"Yes," Latrell replied charily, "but how can we oblige him to cooperate with us? He swears allegiance to no king, no flag, no cause but his own gain. If Uchdryd is a zealot, Albion is a mercenary, a bounty hunter."

A humourless grin emerged on Owein's careworn face. "Then perhaps we could offer him some bounty," he proposed sardonically, as if embracing the inevitability of chaos.

"Yes, Sire, wisely said, Sire," Latrell fumbled, "but allow me to repeat my warning that he cannot be trusted."

Owein's smirk dissolved into a harsh glower. "I have grown accustomed to withholding my trust over the years, Cullen," he remarked opprobriously, letting his glare amplify the ensuing silence. Latrell looked ready to speak when Owein turned back toward the palace and continued walking.

~ Chapter 14 ~

Ever since Urien partook of Gwydir's spring, the forest seemed to be immersed in clear but colourful light, which danced on the river's current to its gentle but perpetual metre. This was no hallucination, though; Urien knew that, just as the burden in his mind was being removed, so the burden on all of the world was being removed. It was as if the universe were looking back at him, meeting his gaze; as if it were sharing in his new birth, marvelling at the oneness of all things that can only be perceived when one is alone with everything. It was the Ancient Way.

Urien knew, though, that this was not the end of his journey, for the walls of Gwydir's cave had revealed to him his fate. The inscriptions led him out of the Ghelt, to the waterless wilderness of Shur – the land beyond the Clovenstone, which marked the boundary of the known world as much as the shores of Tur. Somewhere in that vast oblivion, where not even the brigands of the Mulberry Plains dare tread, lay the Spring of Seeing, the lost holy well of the Third Age.

Shur was not lacking in wells; but, save the holy well, they were full of nothing but dust. According to the legend, they were dug by the Keepers of Alba; but nobody could explain why those first men would choose to abide in the desert, nor indeed why the wells were dry. Some suggested that the wells once gave water, but dried up when the Shai cursed the seas, while others dismissed them as mirages seen by wayward travellers or else as outright fictions. Yet the story which lingered most in the common psyche, particularly among the people of Keldas, Docray, and other nearby towns, was of a reprobate sect of necromancers, who used the pits as portals to an underworld, living beyond their natural lives in the realm of shadow and void.

In this story, the Spring of Seeing was founded by a Priest who dedicated his life to reaching the idolatrous Keepers, imploring them to choose water over thirst, blessing over curse. Whether they repented from their sorcery or still wandered the arid dunes in ghoulish futility was a question that not even folklore claimed to answer, but Urien knew that he would not have been sent to Shur unless there was something still unfinished. How he would survive, he knew not; but, like the Keepers, the choice he now faced was between living to die and dying to live.

The inscriptions had directed Urien to follow the Star of Esa, the Morning Star, the very star followed by Gildas Bedwyr on his pilgrimage across the Jasper Sea. He found the star readily, for its incandescence was like that of the transformed tramp, scintillating and untainted. Though it was only a trace of the Priestly glory, it outshone all other stars, like the sun when it rises; indeed its light was truer than that of the sun, more absolute, for it shone as brightly in the day as it did in the night, and as brightly in the night as it did in the day.

Urien followed the star for a lifetime, an age, an eternity, without path, landmark, or company; yet he thirsted not, for the water of Gwydir's spring sustained him, flowing through him and pouring out of him as if it issued from a wellspring deep within him. Even the desert was imbued with vibrancy, infused with vitality, as if a brand-new world was being born from the bone-dry dust; as if it, too, was being washed and nourished with the waters that move forever between the heights and the depths.

It was weeks before Urien happened upon the first well. He had already resolved to make no allowance for the wicked relics – not to pause, not to peer, not to ponder. According to the inscriptions, no harm could come to him as long as he kept a true bearing towards Esa; for he was the scion of the Old Fathers, walking in the Way invested to them. In any case, he would rather die of thirst than roam the desert thirsty until the end of time – the fate supposedly assigned to those who entered one of the unholy wells. At first, the task seemed easy enough. The well, which lay a stone's throw to his side, appeared as a mere pit, more likely to contain a den of vipers than a source of water. However, as Urien progressed, he realised that his path soon reached a sheer drop, where the undulating dune on which he had been travelling gave way to a broad depression. A minor detour in the direction of the well would afford him a significantly more gradual slope – and thus, he reasoned, a less perilous one.

For a few agonising minutes, Urien's thoughts, eyes, and feet vacillated between the star in the sky and the hole in the ground. Then, as if the world itself was being dismantled, the sky and the ground began to merge. A rude wind began to lift the sand, assembling it into a thick cloud and forging its infinitesimal shards into a spinous whip. It was not long before Urien could see, hear, and feel nothing but the remorseless swarm of pestilential particles, which thrashed his face, infiltrated his lungs, and drove his legs. He lurched spasmodically in whatever direction he was carried until, finally, shelter came into sight. The well, previously a danger, now offered him safety. He clambered into the hole and descended into darkness.

The storm raged until nightfall and through the night. Urien could not determine the contours of the crypt in which he had interred himself, but the circulation of cool air indicated that its belly was wider than its mouth. Urien curled himself up like a foetus, completely blind to the encircling evils that his imagination could, and could not, conceive. He clasped his sword to his bosom, knowing full well that it would not avail him against whatever devilries the Keepers had concocted in this diabolical underworld.

Urien was awoken by the sun, which, upon reaching its daily apex, had breached the narrow gate above him to form a ladder of light, its diamond shafts extending from the heights of the heavens to the depths of the earth, glorifying the particles suspended between. Screening the rays with his hand, Urien peered groggily around the shadowy catacomb. The source of the draft was immediately apparent: though the room was less spacious than he had envisioned, it was surrounded by five evenly spaced thresholds.

With the storm past, Urien had no desire to loiter, let alone reconnoitre. As he prepared to leave, however, he noticed a familiar but forgotten sensation – thirst.

~ Chapter 15 ~

Andras Albion was standing atop the Warden's Tower, overlooking the pride of his family, the price of his loyalty, the prize of his victory. The interchange of arrows had ceased for the night; but come the morning, the Mara would be flowing with the blood of battle. Aelhairn Urien had divested him of his inheritance; now, he would claim it back with interest. The twin cities would be his, no matter the cost.

***

"Forward! Keep pushing forward!"

Not a single stone was visible on the Bridge of the March, the sole passage over the Mara and the bottleneck in the torrent of violence. Bodies – dead, dying, and marching to their deaths – had been piling up since Albion first issued the order. But beyond the squirming sea of red and gold uniforms, amid the fire and brimstone that purged the land and polluted the air, victory was in sight. The King's Men had breached the Durdish defences and were streaming into Glenamara – the first time a Rheg had stepped east of the river since the days of Gorsedd Cadell.

Albion would seize the city with zeal; but he would not stop there. With Glenamara taken, the entire land of Durdich lay open to pillage and plunder. Tiree's terror would spread to Blencathra, Helvellyn, and Mallerstang, fanned into an inferno of fear that would only be quenched by utter ruination. Albion's legions would wring what life remained from this heathen Land; its judgement day had come.

~ Chapter 16 ~

Urien was beset by opposing impulses: although he feared the nameless threats that lurked in the devilish lair, he feared, too, the desiccating exposure of the endless desert. His thirst may well be an enchantment of the cave, an illusion contrived by the Keepers which would vanish when he departed. On the other hand, it could be a hundred leagues until he had another chance to quench it. A brief inspection would not sacrifice the option of escape – should the search prove unsuccessful, he could always return to the atrium and exit via the shaft. Anxiously, he crept through one of the five thresholds that encompassed the room.

Once his eyes adjusted to the dinginess, he found himself in a replica of the first chamber, with the same configuration of encircling doorways, but without the portal to the surface. The air, though, felt cooler and faster, and thus somehow more indicative of water. When he followed the breeze through another opening, he realised that he was ensconced in a beehive of identical, interconnected cells. The scale of the network was impossible to surmise: perhaps it comprised only a handful of rooms, or perhaps it spanned the entire breadth of Shur. Looking back to the first room, Urien could still see the ambient light which emanated from its porthole. Tentatively, he continued to follow the current of air, resolving not to lose the light which marked his way of return.

From cell to cell Urien wandered, acquiescing to what resembled the benevolent Yom of Matzot – the same wind which had led him through the chaos of the forest to the renaissance of the river. Somehow, though, it seemed out of tune, even if it sung the same anthem; and though he never lost the light, he began to doubt it, for it seemed unnaturally constant, failing to dissipate as he ventured further and further through the labyrinth. Eventually his disquiet surpassed his thirst; he thirsted more for escape than he did for water. Resisting the urge to panic, he began to retrace his steps.

As Urien entered the previous chamber, he noticed that the light was now emanating from a different direction; it was a different light. He was positive now that the deception of the well had taken hold; yet the only alternative to pursuing the counterfeit beacon was to fumble vainly through a perpetual midnight. Unnerved, he scurried through the maze as if he were hunting boar in the woods of Tobermory; yet the light grew no brighter and no dimmer.

Urien ran until he could run no more. Instinctively, he clasped his sword, running his thumb over its steel cross-guard. As he looked down on its crown-shaped pommel, he wondered for the first time if he would be capable of using it against himself, to spare himself the fate of the Keepers. But even if he was willing to die, he suspected it would be in vain; for he was already dead, living as a wraith, condemned to rove the underworld alone and unseen until the end of time. This was his lot, his bond, his penance – to dwell forever in the abode of the wicked.

~ Chapter 17 ~

Owein had not been in his parents' chamber since his mother died. His father's second disappearance had impelled him here, to seek, though he knew not what he hoped to find.

The room was musty and dusty, as if the same dead air had filled it for an age. He drifted over to his mother's chiffonier, atop of which lay her jewellery stand. The ornaments were modest for a queen; she had never been one to flaunt the wealth at her disposal, contenting herself with a few items of sentimental value. Owein picked up her wedding ring, the cornerstone of the collection, which he had himself placed there some twenty years ago, shortly after Coira's funeral. The Doves of Shekinah, symbolising the blessing of the Shai on the Old Kingdom before they departed from the world, still glided through their golden promises to become each other, returning to complete the eternal circle.

Returning the ring to the cabinet, Owein noticed an object which he had not seen before: an oyster shell fastened to a necklace of rope. The trinket was conspicuously out of place: not only was its crudeness unbefitting for a queen's wardrobe, but the oyster suggested Aramean provenance. A souvenir from his father's excursion, Owein presumed; and yet somehow it seemed more valuable, more meaningful, than all the gold in Rheged. Urien had been absent for Coira's death; indeed, it was his absence that, Owein believed, was ultimately to blame for her fatal madness. The keepsake was evidence that he felt remorse, if not regret; that he understood the cost of his sainthood, a cost which could not be paid with expensive wares.

If the ring reminded Owein that Rheged was a Kingdom, the necklace reminded him that it was, once again, without a king. The kingling which did reside possessed neither sword nor queen – and would not until the line of Aelhairn had ended. It may never end, thought Owein, for Urien's body may never be found; he would either live forever in the New World or die alone in the Old, succumbing to the inexorable process of decay that held the world in bondage. Without a body, there could be no funeral, and Owein's father would continue to be king long after he had passed beyond the seven seas. Rheged, too, was going the way of all the earth, ready to be devoured by the host of scavengers who already lurked in the shadows.

While the Old Kingdom had fallen long ago, the New seemed a world away. Owein began to realise that he must reach that world.

~ Chapter 18 ~

Dahaka had finished supping with his wife. They ate what all the Qa ate, various combinations of seafood and seaweed; lived as all the Qa lived, in a dry-slate hut with their children and the husband's parents; and dreamt as all the Qa dreamt, of a land that they had never known.

"Why do you not advance the army, qa of my qa?" Dahaka Qam asked as she nursed their newborn child. "Bedwas and Bassien Ram have committed themselves to the March. Morraine and Beggerin are scoundrels, but not fools: Turihal now lies open to our forces. We finally have the chance to break free from this prison of rock."

Dahaka took a sip from his glass of kelp liqueur, letting the vapours permeate his airways, appreciating its subtle notes of ashwood and sumac. "It's the sea," he reflected as he gazed into the spirit. With its deep, charcoal hues and its rich, protean bitterness, it was a microcosm of its origin – the endless waters of the Onyx Sea, which forever separated Tur from the islands of Qahal. "The waves are calmer. The water is clearer. The fishermen say the gulls are moving their nests to the Yanahal."

Dahaka Qam bobbed the baby up and down as it began to cry. "And how do you read these signs, qa of my qa?"

Dahaka looked up from the chalice. "Aelhairn Raman has returned from exile," he replied, consciously leaving her question unanswered.

Dahaka Qam stopped rocking the baby. "You think that this Rhega is the Peaceful One?"

"I know not, qa of my qa," Dahaka responded with troubled sincerity, "but what if he is?"

Dahaka Qam stood up with the baby and began cradling him back and forth, soothing his cries with affectionate shushes. Once he was pacified, she spoke to her husband softly so as not to undo her efforts. "You are Dahaka Ram, soon to be Dahaka, the Chosen One of our people. You must seek wisdom like a pearl; and you must find it." Delicately, Dahaka Qam carried the baby out of the room and towards his crib.

Dahaka took another sip of the liqueur. As he began to lower the glass, the squalls of Dahaka Raman could once again be heard, followed by the tired sigh and loving consolations of Dahaka Qam. He swigged the remaining liquid, set the glass on the table, and went to help his wife.

~ Chapter 19 ~

"You are the only councillor that I trust, Malvern," Owein confided to the stout general as they strolled through the Garden of Shemesh. "Apart from the High Commander, of course – but then as a landless functionary he has nothing to gain from betrayal, unlike Emrys, Cullen, and the rest of them. He is invulnerable to their plots and wiles – but also, I fear, oblivious of them."

"What have I to gain, Your Highness?" Brennus rejoined humorously as they approached the royal cemetery, surrounded by a mausoleum of hawthorn hedges. "I've already betrayed my age, and my punishment is coming due – though perhaps my cunning will be remembered," he added, stopping at the limestone memorial which stood at the head of the burial ground.

Owein scrutinised the cenotaph, which honoured those who had died in the service of Rheged. "You knew my father when he was a boy. Tell me, what was he like?"

Brennus crimped the corner of his mouth with a half-smile as he consulted his memory. "He was much like you, if I may presume to say so, Your Highness – quick-witted and strong-willed. Once he was engaged in a task, he would perform it wholeheartedly – but the difficulty lay in engaging him. Teaching him swordsmanship was no mean feat when he would rather spend his time building imaginary worlds in his bedchamber."

Suddenly losing interest in the monument, Owein recommended the walk. "Do you believe the tales, Brennus?" he asked, reluctant to ask himself the question and unsure which response he desired.

Brennus shuffled back into motion. "'The tales', Highness?"

"My father's 'imaginary worlds', as you called them. You know," Owein expounded, waving his hand dismissively through the air, "the Shai, Dalriada." He paused before continuing in a more solemn tone. "The prophecies."

Brennus scrunched his face as he contemplated a response. "I believe in your father, Sire, as I believe in you."

"I wish I shared your faith, Brennus," Owein lamented, diverting himself with the steady pendulum of his own own gait.

"If I may speak openly, Sire…" Brennus intimated respectfully.

"Come, Malvern," Owein adjured, once again swiping his hand through the air. "I would have summoned Morraine if I had desired flummery and prevarication. Speak."

"My belief is born of fear as much as faith," Brennus confided soberly. "Unless your father's judgement is true, and unless you accomplish what he importunes of you, the Kingdom may fall."

Owein continued walking in silence, once again watching his feet as they alternated between left and right, backward and forward. "Indeed," he eventually affirmed, "it is already falling. You may have nothing to gain, Malvern; but I fear that the Kingdom may already be lost."

~ Chapter 20 ~

The night was perfectly poised. A crepuscular candelabra of pale stars emitted just enough light for the soldiers to perform their maneuver without alerting their prey, who slumbered obviously in the town below. To be sure, the cliff was steep – so steep, in fact, that it sloped back on itself, like the face of a cresting wave. But the nets were strong, woven to bear the bountiful catches of the sea beyond the sea; and though they had not been fully filled since the exodus of Qahal, they had, like the souls they now suspended, withstood the weight of time immemorial.

The road to Ravenshield was guarded night and day; but it wound around the mountain, diverting for miles to avoid the precipitous overhang. A direct descent from the Helm had only been accomplished by those destined for death, willingly or otherwise. This time, death itself would descend from the precipice, raining down on the city like fire from on high. This was the will of the Qa that beats within the earth, the Qa of all Qa; it was the destiny of Turahal.

That, at least, was what Dahaka told himself as he peered down to the craggy talus where the first of his troops had landed. He feared not for their welfare; indeed, he envied those who would escape this life of rock to dwell forever in the Heartland. But his own heart wrenched, for he had brought war to the man who, in his heart, he knew to be the Peaceful One – the one who would pacify the Qa that beats within the earth, so that the sea would cease its wrenching, so that the people of

Qahal could return to the home they never had.

Dahaka assured himself that his hand had been forced. Unlike the kings of Turahal, he cared not for conquest and imperium, and nor did any of the Qa. As in the days of Cadell, when they repelled the forces of Rheged on these very mountains, their concern merely to preserve their bloodline; indeed, the days of Cadell had returned. Word had reached Dahaka that Andras Albion had broken through at the Mara and now marauded unchecked through the Marches of the Glen. The miscreant Warden would not stop until all of Durdich was subdued; and indeed, he would not stop even then. The kingdoms of Turahal were collapsing, and the Qa must not be buried in the ruins; when Albion reached Aram, they must not find themselves with their backs against the Onyx Sea.

In any case, this was not Urien's war, but Owein's; and unlike his father, the son of the Peaceful One had not seen the other side of the sea. The first in the line of Bedwas would not accept the Way of Peace even if it were offered to him.

At least, that was what Dahaka told himself.

~ Chapter 21 ~

Owein followed the path of his father, the path of the Old Fathers. The mounting threat of the East and the consequent irrelevance of the West had prevented him from ever travelling the length of the Royal Road, though he had often traced it on his map with wistful curiosity.

A convenient result was that he would not be recognised once he left the purlieus of Wetherstag; but it was only then that the full repercussions of his neglect became evident. The further he journeyed from the capital, the more destitute the country had become – evidence of the Kingdom's chronic decline and a portent of its impending collapse.

When he reached Oxenfen, that inauspicious juncture between order and anarchy, Owein diverged from his father's precedent.Whereas Urien had risked the endless, lawless void of the Mulberry Plains, Owein held to the safety of the northern road. With the survival of the Kingdom hanging in the balance, he could take no chances; he would make for the terminus of Watendlath and enter the Ghelt from the east. To compensate for the longer distance, he would ride through the night, with the intention of replacing his horse once it showed signs of foundering.

Owein was grateful not to be suffering the sinister Plains, which seemed to swallow the sun as it set; yet as he tracked the outer rim like a dog lurking for scraps, the table still taunted him with its empty regale, offering him only bitter wind and insipid repetition. He had hoped to procure victuals before reaching Brambia, but the settlements along the weathered bypass were dispirited shells, deserted by traders and despoiled by raiders. The few inhabitants not immured within primitive shanties exhibited hollow frowns and hardened scowls, assuming that his presence spelled detriment but too numb to do anything more than shrink inwards, brace themselves, and wait for death.

Owein was delirious by the time Watendlath came into sight, but a welcome sight it was. Amid what seemed like a never-ending night, the lonesome town was an oasis of light. As he rallied, however, it only seemed to retreat, as if it were fixed to the horizon like a fallen star. Then, in the blink of an eye, he was there, his warhorse swaying with exhaustion as it straggled to the village common, where it proceeded to swill from a cattle trough. Owein dismounted blunderingly, a rush of blood to his semi-conscious brain leaving him teetering on his half-dead legs until, with another blink, he lay prostrate, breathing in the evening earth.

Another blink, and Owein was awake – still lying, but now supine, on what felt like a haystack in what looked, smelled, and sounded like a barn. He lay motionless as he peered through the air, punctured by delicate shafts peeping through narrow slits, revealing minute debris suspended in the stillness. Before his dilated eyes could adjust, an unseen portal sprung ajar, inundating the barn with daylight. In the doorway stood an indistinguishable figure, whose modest silhouette was surpassed by its towering shadow.

"Ah, y're awake!" cheeped the figure before crossing the threshold, revealing a ruddy aspect and a head of unruly red hair. "There's some tea's been brewed – oh and Edda's griddlin' some kipp'rs, if that would take y'r fancy." Still dazed, Owein failed to comprehend the provincial accent – which, after two weeks of nomadic solitude, nevertheless sounded like birdsong. "I know it's not very, you know, kingly," the sprightly lad continued, "but them kipp'rs is mighty flav'rsome, if I don't say so myself."

Owein sat up as his consciousness returned. "Tea," he finally managed, immediately discovering a drought in his mouth. "Yes, tea – thank you."

Beaming with delight, the ginger hobbledehoy nodded enthusiastically before bowing bashfully. "Be back in a jiffy," he spluttered before scampering towards the doorway, only to halt in his tracks and rotate backwards. "And the kipp'rs?"

"Oh – yes, please," Owein replied cordially, removing a stalk of hay from his scruffy mane. As the stranger scuttled out of sight, Owein alighted from his manger, scratching the spots on his back where the straw had pierced his tunic. He moseyed over to the stable to find two grade horses alongside his royal steed, which was masticating contentedly. He, too, was famished, though the reek of the adjacent pigsty served to dampen his appetite.

Owein moved to the sunlit doorway. The light was ripe and mature, weathered and wisened by love and loss, content with a life well-lived and grateful for a life worth living. As he stepped into the dying daybreak, he saw his amiable waiter trotting toward him over a foot-worn courtyard, across from which lay a quaint, ramshackle cottage. A whiff of velvet smoke rose daintily from its crooked chimney, which poked through a patchwork of tousled thatches.

"Beggin' y'r pard'n, Y'r Highness," the energetic youth blurted while still en route, "but we – me 'n' Edda, that is – we thought p'rhaps you'd

85

rath'r have y'r breakfast in the house instead of the barn." He had nearly finished his suggestion by the time he arrived. "It's no palace, you know, but it's sure nicer 'n' 'at ol' barn."

Owein couldn't help but grin. "That would be lovely, thank you."

"I'm Mungo, by the way," the freckle-faced companion disclosed, avidly proffering his calloused hand. "Mungo Caldbeck."

~ Chapter 22 ~

"Don't mind Mungo – he knows everything there is to know, but he's as foolish as a calf." Edda Leavenmeal was dispensing tea at the rickety table where Owein was seated, along with Mungo and a crusty senior who Owein presumed to be Mungo's father. Both were staring at him fixedly, but whereas Mungo appeared as if he might burst with excitement, his elder maintained a leery scowl. "Awful sorry bout puttin' you up in that stinkin' old barn," Edda continued. "You were dead as a dormouse when we found you, and it wasn't no doddle tryin' t'move ya. Would've needed a Priest to get you up them stairs."

"Not to worry, madam," Owein replied, unsure where to direct his own eyes. "I'm extremely grateful for your hospitality."

Edda looked away and touched her chest dramatically, as if she was fainting. "Oh – 'madam' – how flatterin'! D'ya hear that, Gav'r?"

"We're not accustomed to outsid'rs in these parts," the curmudgeon grumbled gruffly. "Anyone in their right mind would be suspicious of someone comin' up this way – fancy trimmin's notwithstandin'."

"Don't mind Gav'r," Edda remarked glibly. "He's been bitt'r ev'r since he lost our best hog in a game of check'rs last week." Gaver muttered grouchily at the anecdote before retrieving a pipe and matches from his breast pocket. "Quite a both'r it was too," Edda elaborated, "we'd been fatt'nin' him up for wint'r – hadn't we Gav'r?"

"As you keep remindin' me," Gaver replied sourly, igniting his pipe.

"Anyway, looks like we'll be havin' kipp'rs three times a day till spring comes," Edda mused as she returned the teapot to a homely kiln, where the cured fish were being smoked over a stack of apple wood. "And that's assumin' the riv'r don't ice ov'r."

"Which it always do," Gaver interjected between puffs.

"In which case it'll be horse meat for you, you pathetic gambl'r." Gaver repeated his string of incoherent chuntering before executing a series of agitated puffs. "Speakin' of kipp'rs, looks like they're just about ready," Edda chirped as she retrieved the cold-smoked herrings, the aroma of which had been tormenting Owein's querulous stomach. "No need for manners," she instructed as she laid the offering in the middle of the table. "Best get 'em 'fore Gav'r eats 'em all up." Gaver declined to acknowledge the jeer.

"I'd like to say a pray'r before we eat," announced Mungo, having yet to say a word. Gaver humphed grumpily.

"Oh, Mungo, you and your religion," Edda fussed. "Our guest must be starvin'.'"

"No, madam, it's quite alright," Owein politely affirmed, despite the furious protest of his appetite. Mungo beamed at the assurance, which he interpreted as definitive authorisation to proceed. Closing his eyes, he commenced his recital:

> "Elah, our et'rnal Fath'r, who created the world;
>
> Elah, our holy Fath'r, who judges the world;
>
> Elah, our gracious Fath'r, who deliv'rs the world –
>
> Sanctify this day the land, which You have blessed;
>
> Sanctify this day Y'r people, whom You have called;
>
> And sanctify this day our nourishment, which You have provided."

"Now, Mungo, where did you learn such a graceful pray'r?" Edda inquired as Gaver served himself from the platter. Owein was not accustomed to doing so, but the sensation of an empty stomach was just as foreign to a king of Rheged. His sense of propriety overridden by his bodily instincts, he shamelessly followed Gaver's example.

"From Nana," Mungo replied.

"Of course," Edda recalled, turning to Owein. "His grandmoth'r – Elah bless her – she was my second cousin. A Wakebarrow if ever there was one, she was. She told him all sorts of stories about the Priests. Talks about 'em all the time, he does."

Gaver submitted a token groan.

"You must know all the pray'rs, Y'r Highness," Mungo suggested to

Owein, "what with bein' king an' all."

"'Y'r Highness'? 'King'?" Edda interposed bewilderedly, her eyes darting between Mungo and Owein. "What on Elah's good earth are you talkin' about, Mungo?"

~ Chapter 23 ~

Conventional histories of Tur began with the establishment of the Old Kingdom, when, according to popular myth, the departing Priests entrusted their legacy to the Old Fathers – Rhain, Rhiell, and Rhodd, after whom the Home Counties of Rheged were named. In more peripheral areas, lay-legend spanned farther back, to the first saint, Gwydir Aspatria, chosen by the Shai to conceive the Ancient Way of Dalriada – the Way which the Old Fathers were chosen to preserve. Yet the same tale held that the Shai had arrived in Tur an entire age before this event; and when it came to the question of what transpired in the intervening period, even the most fantastical of sagas were curiously silent.

It was generally imagined that the Priests had simply confined themselves to the edges and wilds of the continent, dealing seldom with the aboriginal Keepers of Alba until the appointed time. The only explicit reference to the Third Age, however, was found in the little-known legend of blessing, according to which the Shai had sanctified the springs, rivers, and lakes of Tur immediately upon reaching its rugged shores – the same shores which they would leave two ages later, scourging the seas in their wake. The condemnation of the outer waters was thus preceded by the consecration of the inner, which continued to flow through the veins and arteries of earth and man, nurturing and nourishing the land and its people until the latter day, when the former things will pass away.

The priestly blessing remained invisible to those who neglected to seek it; but there were certain places where even those who were blind could not help but see.

"How did you know I was coming, Mungo?" It was the question that Owein had been longing to ask all morning. Despite planning to resume his journey immediately after breakfast, he had remained in Edda's cenacle for several hours, listening to the ebullient if unpolished Mungo and answering the obsequious if inquisitive Edda. To his perceptible chagrin, Gaver had been sent to slaughter their best pig, which, at Edda's persistent behest, he had summarily skinned, impaled, and trussed above the flaming kiln. Owein wondered how an animal could smell so nauseating when alive but so appetising when cooked.

Mungo leapt at the invitation to elaborate. "Back home – Hartsop, that's me home, that is – they said in the Roundhouse that King Urien had come back. I knew right away to come here – to Wat'rend, I mean, to Aunt Edda and Uncle Gaver's house – 'cause it says in Myrddin's stories that the new King would come here."

Gaver grunted at the mention of the fabled bard, who himself appeared in a handful of legends impossibly disconnected by time and space. Even Edda could not contain her incredulity. "Myrddin?" she entreated quizzically. "Why, Mungo, don't you know he's make-believe?"

Mungo, refusing to countenance the suggestion, proceeded to recite the relevant passage:

"The King of Peace will come again,

Back from Shailoh he will come.

To Wat'r's End his son will come,

To make the world new again."

The room fell silent, save the erratic crackle of roasting pork. Though recent events had compelled Owein to reconsider the prophecies, their quotation evoked the resentment he still carried toward his one-time father – the so-called 'King of Peace', who, for the second time, had abandoned his son on the eve of war.

"I am here to save Rheged, not Tur," he eventually enounced, suppressing a melee of frustration and embarrassment.

Gaver, apparently sobered by Mungo's revelation, rejoined with unexpected astuteness. "There was a time, Y'r Highness, when the twain w're one and the same."

Chapter 24

"Yes, I've already heard about Ravenshield!" Brennus turned to another of the officials who swarmed around him, buzzing him with information. "Yes, for Elyon's sake, I know about Owein!"

Since the second king vanished, chaos had reigned in Wetherstag. According to the law of the land, interim rule should pass to General Brennus in the absence of royalty; yet the particulars of such a situation remained unclear, especially during wartime. As chains of command and lines of communication tangled around each other in a cobweb of confusion, an army of civil administrators scrambled helter-skelter to deal with the unfolding conflict.

Brennus finally snapped. "Hold your confounded tongues, all of you!" he yelled at the mob, which instantly quietened. "Where in the Wilderness of Shur is Cullen Latrell?"

"Here," answered the quarry himself. He was standing directly behind Brennus, who duly turned to face him.

"Cullen, we must summon the council at once." Brennus began to shuffle towards the exit, flicking his hand to indicate that his addressee should follow. "Albion must be recalled forthwith to shore up our defences. Nothing but a straight, unguarded road now lies between us and the Aramites."

"Of course, His Highness," Latrell replied guardedly as they left the building, acknowledging the general's vicarious authority, "but Emrys

Morraine has urgently requested your presence. Perhaps we should attend to him first."

Baffled, Brennus stopped in his tracks. "Morraine? I thought he was in Tabor caring for his sickly aunt."

"He returned late last night," Latrell replied charily. "He possesses some crucial news which he wills to share with you."

"Never mind his news," Brennus bristled. "He has some explaining to do. Where is he?"

"In the Rose Chapel, His Highness," Latrell answered casually, referring to the abandoned sanctuary at the end of the Garden of Shemesh.

"The Rose Chapel? What in the Twelve Seas is he doing there? Praying?" Brennus chuckled sardonically at the thought before brusquely discarding the issue. "Ah, what it does matter. I could use the fresh air anyway. That posse of clerks has nearly driven me to madness. You'd think this was some sort of provincial government, the way things are run. Come," he enjoined, recommencing his laboured waddle. "Let us see what Morraine has to say. His tidings had better be fair, mind you – we've had enough misfortune for one day."

Latrell strained to suppress his satisfaction. "Very well, His Highness."

~ Chapter 25 ~

Having bid his hosts farewell, Owein was leading his revitalised stallion out of the courtyard towards the road – the road to the Ghelt, to the Ashness River, and to Gwydir's cave. To Owein's perplexity, however, Mungo had followed him, and showed no sign of desisting.

Once he reached the road, Owein turned to his unsolicited chaperon and extended his hand. "It was a pleasure to make your acquaintance, Mungo Caldbeck," he imparted courteously, hoping that the tacit dismissal would be understood. "May your kindness be rewarded many times over."

Mungo was aghast. "I'm comin' with you, Y'r Highness," he exclaimed, oblivious to the impertinence of his assertion, not to mention his failure to acknowledge the king's gesture of appreciation.

Owein checked himself before responding. "I appreciate your eagerness to help, young sir, but I'm afraid it's out of the question." Heedless of his own patronising tone, he continued, "The urgency of my business does not allow for dependents."

Mungo was initially crestfallen, but, as if unearthing an inspiration, he raised his lustrous eyes from the dusty ground. "Do you remember Myrddin's stories, Sire?"

Owein did remember, now that Mungo had reminded him; but his bitter reflex to the mythological, which had been regularly triggered in the past few hours, continued to bite, this time through his sense of civility. "Do you presume to be the Acolyte, the Great Servant of the Old Fathers?" he challenged scornfully, as if conducting an inquisition.

"I don't presume nothin', Your Highness," Mungo replied with irreproachable sincerity. "I was only sayin' that you're gonna' need someone who knows the prophecies, seein' as how you're fulfillin' them an' all. And you'll need someone who knows the land," he added with a disarming smile, as if touting the one credential of which he was truly proud. "I know the land bett'r 'n I know meself."

Owein was embarrassed. The notion that Mungo represented the reincarnation of Elyon's Servant had already developed in his own psyche, arousing a nettlesome disquietude which he had projected onto the subject. The truth was that this unworldly sprite astounded Owein. The Brambian's whole way of being was deferential, genuine, and magnanimous; indeed, contrary to Owein's insinuation, he seemed not to presume anything at all. By the same token, however, he had given no special treatment to Owein. Whereas Edda had been frantically fawning, sportively sardonic, and benevolently condescending towards her respective guests, Mungo's comportment had been uniformly chivalrous. He respected all people, and indeed all things; but he was no respecter of persons.

"Very well," Owein finally yielded, attempting to maintain a businesslike bearing, "perhaps you'll be of some use in locating Gwydion's cave; but we shall be leaving forthwith."

"I've already packed," Mungo replied buoyantly. "I've not got much anyways – jus' this old knapsack". As if advertising his readiness, he shrugged his shoulder to reposition the bag's ropen strap, which he clasped intently with both hands. "Oh – and I've got me own 'orse – well, she's me Uncle Frigg's, but he let me borrow 'er, 'e did."

"Very well," Owein reiterated, this time unable to restrain a faint grin. "Best go and tack her up then."

Mungo, who seemed never to merely walk, scuttered off to the barn.

***

The duo had barely left the village, but already Owein had received a comprehensive education in Turian folklore – the subtle yet crucial differences between Brambian and Rhegish mythologies; the paramount importance of all four interpretations of the Lindisfarne Chronicles; the various ways in which the genealogies of the Ula and the Una could be reconciled. Owein had responded to the rambling yarns with open questions, for the commentary was a welcome contrast to the vapid seclusion of his journey thus far. Nevertheless, he blenched at the constant reminder of his father's inexplicable conversion.

"Tell me about your family, Mungo," Owein finally interjected, purposing to change the subject. "Have you siblings? Children of your own perhaps?"

"Nah, me 'n' Nana are the only Caldbecks left," Mungo replied after a brisk shake of the head, more nostalgic than mournful, "exceptin' if you count them Coldbecks up in the Rye. Me folks died in the Great Famine. Nana says it was Gorsedd Cadell's doin' – the famine, I mean.

Says he made us give up all our food for the soldiers. Says he made us keep workin' the ground, never lettin' it rest. Eventually it gave up — that's what happens when you don't let the ground rest. Was years 'fore it was fert'l again."

Despite his attempt to initiate a lighter conversation, Owein was riled by the mention of his ancestral bane. "I, too, have reason to hate Cadell, for he was also responsible for the death of my kin."

Mungo appeared disconcerted, as if he were struggling to digest Owein's statement. "Beggin' y'r pardon, Sire," he rejoined, "but I don't hate no one, 'part from maybe that Balder Appletree after he's drank more than he should. Like I says, the land gives back what you put in — that Cadell must've been awful miserable considerin' all the awful things he done. Besides, I'll see me ma and pa in the New World. That's why you're here — isn't it, Sire? The New World, I mean."

Owein was once again astounded by his candid ally, whose exceptional kindheartedness exposed the hypocrisy, malignancy, and insanity of hate. The countryside itself seemed to confirm the testimony: the meticulous mosaic of odd-stone walls, the neat rows of upturned dirt, the elaborate network of overgrown paths — here was an organic order undisturbed by a lawless world, a divine rhythm unbroken by the world's imbalance. Owein took several deep, nourishing breaths before uttering his verdict. "Yes, the New World. The Ancient Way will be restored."

Mungo's face gleamed with joy as if the sun itself were shining through him.

~ Chapter 26 ~

Malvern Brennus and Cullen Latrell were approaching the Rose Chapel, so named for its arrangement of elliptical galleries surrounding a central nave. "I was only a bairn when I last visited this kirk," Brennus related wistfully as they reached the litter of dilapidated gravestones that bedecked the churchyard, flushed in the unsullied solstice. "I used to hide here from my inebriate father. A good man he was, a true servant of the realm, but the Gates of Golgotha would open when he took to drink. Aye, many a cold and sleepless night I spent on the pews of this kirk, whimpering like a milksop, begging Elyon to save my mother from the old man's fist. My prayers were answered, in a way," Brennus soliloquised as they eased open the arthritic door, "Malvern Lanarth died of the bilious fever when I had but eight years of age. It was the drink that killed him."

Emrys Morraine emerged from one of the sanctuaries as they stepped into the nave. "Death has a way of mocking us, does it not, Malvern?" Even his tinny, pinched voice ricocheted through the outer galleries, crisscrossing the nave from all directions.

Before Brennus could respond, the door thundered shut behind him. He swung around his burdensome belly as Latrell, who stood forbiddingly before the exit, pulled back the inset of his cloak to advertise a sword which hung from his waist. Brennus instinctively reached for his own.

"Don't make this difficult, Malvern," Morraine fussed theatrically, enjoying his own show. "Even if your old bones managed to vanquish the two of us, an entire patrol would be waiting for you in the Garden."

Brennus's bushy moustache and bushier eyebrows gave the appearance of a constant scowl, but this time the expression was genuine. "Owein would have removed you long ago, you venomous snake, had he not relied so heavily on your armies!"

"The cardinal rule of survival is to make yourself indispensable to those with power," Morraine cooed superciliously. "Unfortunately, my old friend, you have broken that rule."

"You may attain power, Emrys, but power over what?" Brennus stepped towards Morraine, whose smugly draped eyelids marginally recoiled. Latrell began to draw his sword, but Morraine raised his index finger as if to warn him otherwise. "Soon there will be no blood left for you to suck," Brennus continued. "Surely you are better eating from the king's hand than overturning the table and spoiling the fare. What game are you playing?"

"Quite a simple one, really," Morraine answered boastfully, "more like checkers than chess. Rheged will destroy Durdich, and Aram will destroy Rheged. Only the Qa will be left – and I've found them to be much easier to deal with than the Turians."

"And what of Albion?" Brennus fumed through gritted teeth. "You will still have to deal with him."

"Yes," Morraine conceded airily, once again raising his finger as if to lecture a child, "but that's where those indispensable armies come into play. Albion's forces will be scattered and depleted by the time he conquers the East. I, on the other hand, will command the entire King's Army. Owein's departure could not have been more fortuitous."

"Treason!" Brennus exploded, overcome with righteous wrath. He was still unsheathing his own blade when Latrell's came thrusting through his thorax, inducing his spine to spasm and his face to wan. Paralysed by the impalement, he gaped at the protruding skewer until Latrell withdrew it, using his free hand as leverage against the general's fleshy frame. Brennus fell to the floor with a guttural gargle.

"Thank you, Cullen," said Morraine impassively, producing a handkerchief to wipe a splatter of blood from his face. Just then, the door swung open as a half-dozen troops stormed into the chapel, surrounding the nave. "We have the situation under control," Morraine assured them. When the soldiers failed to respond, he ruffled. "What's the matter with you? Don't you know a dead man when you see one? The deed is already done – now be gone!"

"I'm afraid you have broken the second rule of survival, my old friend," Latrell inserted waggishly, "do unto others before they do unto you."

~ Chapter 27 ~

"This is the Way!" Mungo hollered back to Owein, who cast a pitiful figure slouched beneath his sodden hood. The rain had descended throughout the night, activating the soil and churning up the immanent fragrance of fruitfulness. In contrast to Owein, Mungo had not been demoralised by the experience; on the contrary, he seemed even more buoyant than usual, every now and again casting his face to the generous sky as if giving thanks in a way that only a farmer would understand.

"Where are you leading us?" Owein grumbled from his sorry tent, his noble civilities eroded by discomfort. "By my reckoning, we should have reached the Ghelt before nightfall; yet here we are, hours thence, wallowing in mud and cow dung."

"We're not goin' to the Ghelt, Y'r Highness," Mungo remarked ingenuously. "That's not the Way."

"What are you playing at, Mungo Caldbeck?" Owein snarled. "Of course it's the bloody way. What else of import could there be in this confounded slough?"

"The Rock of Bethelah," Mungo replied, interpreting the question as genuine. "Don't you know the stories?"

Owein had never heard of such an object. Nevertheless, over the past three days his mythological literacy had been definitively outmatched, and his assumptions regarding Mungo's intelligence consistently overturned. He decided to remain silent this time.

It was not long before his trust was rewarded. "Here it is!" Mungo suddenly exclaimed, leaping off his nag and rushing to the centre of the field, where an unremarkable slab of granite was lodged upright in the saturated earth. "The Rock of Bethelah! Come on, Y'r Highness," he hooted endearingly with an energetic wave. Owein duly obliged, but chose to stay on his horse while he negotiated the waterlogged glebe.

Mungo held up his lantern to the inconspicuous monument as Owein approached. "Me Uncle Frigg says there used to be a roundhouse here," he related. "Now there's just this stone."

"Is it a tombstone?" Owein asked languorously, struggling to muster interest.

"'Course not, Y'r Highness," Mungo replied. "It's a mem'ry stone." Owein vaguely recalled the term, but could not pinpoint the context. Mungo construed his lack of reaction as nescience. "It tells of the past."

"But there's no writing on it," Owein observed glumly.

"There used to be," Mungo replied, "but it's all worn off. Least that's what me Uncle Frigg says. His farm's just down yonder." Mungo pointed across the field, his gesture almost imperceptible through the dense downpour and the dim dusk. "Heron House. Been in the family since the Olden Times, that farm has."

His patience exhausted, Owein refused to entertain the digression. "How is this rock supposed to help us?"

Mungo shrugged his shoulders. "All's I know is that this is where we're supposed to be."

Owein assessed the situation cerebrally, as if he were directing a military operation. "It won't avail us to trudge through this muck with no daylight and no objective," he determined from the loftiness of his steed. "We shall camp here until daybreak, whereupon we will review our situation. That humble coppice may provide us with some degree of shelter," he declared, indicating towards the edge of the field.

"Nana always says there's nothin' like a good night's sleep for clearin' things up," Mungo warbled.

Owein found Mungo's indefatigable alacrity both vexatious and comforting. "Including the weather, we shall hope."

***

The muddied wayfarers had barely retired an hour when the thunder first erupted in the distance, reverberating across the horizon as if ground and sky had been torn asunder. What began as a solitary war-drum was soon accompanied by a resounding percussion, which encircled the field as if heralding Armageddon. The storm became yet more calamitous – its tempo faster, its pitch deeper, its articulation louder – as the onslaught began. A barrage of watery arrows, fired by the advancing legion of pressure, wind, and heat, foreshadowed the climactic strike: jagged scythes of fiery light, which ignited the night to forge instantaneous stairways from Heaven to earth.

The spectacle was all the more fearsome viewed from within the woodgrove, the whirling spokes of which shattered the oncoming blitz into myriad fragments, enveloping the defenseless prey in a cobweb of shadows and scintillations. It was not until lightning struck their deciduous shelter, though, that Owein and Mungo were forced to flee.

"We can't leave!" cried Mungo over the cataclysm. "We can't leave the mem'ry stone!"

"We will be consumed if we stay here!" Owein shouted back as he began to untie his stallion, which was now as berserk as the storm that had spooked it.

After a moment of frenzied deliberation, Mungo turned and starting racing towards the stone at the centre of the field. "Then we'll have to take it with us!" he called back.

Owein, failing to control his bedevilled beast and no longer concerned with the state of his vesture, followed in express remonstration: "There's no way on Tur that we'll be able to lift it, let alone carry it!" Undeterred in his errand, Mungo, though failing to lift the boulder, succeeded in wrestling it to the ground, uprooting its unseen underbelly from its undefiled bed. As Owein arrived, a protracted sky-blaze illuminated the resting fundament, now exposed to the raging firmament. "Mungo," Owein called to his fellow refugee, who continued to exert himself in the mud. "Stop. There's writing on it."

Mungo immediately obeyed, scrambling on blistered hands and soiled knees to verify the observation. With the eagerness of a pup at mealtime, he read out the resurrected epitaph between peals of thunder and flashes of lightning.

"The Righteous King must trust the star
Which guided saints to lands afar.
Far across waters must he walk
Until he reaches solid rock.
From holy bedrock to Gerar,
Go! and consummate Heaven's earthen wedlock."

Owein, reverting to his martial persona, gazed pensively into the tempestuous air as the precipitation included him in its seminal journey, cascading down his head and streaming from his limbs. "So be it," he declared, aloof from his perilous situation. "Mungo, retrieve your horse. We have our destination."

The aide-de-camp instinctively obeyed, but completed only a few strides in the direction of their erstwhile shelter before performing an about-face. With the same doggedness he had exhibited in felling the stone, he presently endeavoured to set it upright in its original substratum. Owein, recognising the obligation of the task, duly assisted until the memorial had been reinstated.

The highborn prince, now resembling a lowly farmhand, supplicated his brother-in-labour: "Come, Mungo; you must lead us to Gerar."

~ Chapter 28 ~

Owein had been compelled to release his thoroughbred, which the night's weather had traumatised beyond recovery. Both passengers now rode together on Mungo's seasoned grey, which, by contrast, had remained phlegmatic throughout the episode. The storm had abated, the night had receded, and their raiment had nearly dried as they aspired towards the ascendant sun.

"Reckon it'll take us 'bout three days to reach Gerar," Mungo counselled spontaneously. "This ol' mare – Morag's her name – she ain't the quickest, but she'll keep goin' and goin' till Shailoh comes. 'Fore me Uncle Frigg bought 'er at auction she was a packhorse – may have covered this very route, now that I think about it. Doesn't need hardly any food or sleep."

"Alas, I have not been endowed with such miraculous powers," Owein droned wearily. "The horse may be able to continue indefinitely, but I'm afraid I shall require sustenance before the day is out."

"Not a problem, Y'r Highness," Mungo responded with his usual gaiety, before ferreting out a mushy biscuit from the saddlebag. "Our rations are soaked through, but they're still fine for eatin'." Owein accepted the offering reluctantly, staring at the mangled mass in the vain hope that it would transubstantiate into a freshly baked loaf. "As for sleepin', feel free to take a kip. Like I says, I know this land bett'r 'n I know meself." Owein was growing accustomed to being simultaneously charmed and irked by his incorruptible comrade. "So how about y'rself, Y'r Highness," Mungo continued, evidently not intending for his discussant to retire anytime soon. "Do you have any family? Oth'r than y'r fath'r, I mean."

Owein replied wistfully. "My mother passed when I was a young man – a younger man, at least. I have no wife or children." His woeful mien betrayed a tinge of spite. "Thanks to my father's futile obsession with making peace, I am irrevocably betrothed to Ayla Breaca. She is sister of my adversary, Bassien Dunragit."

"So why haven't you married her yet, if you don't mind me askin', Y'r Highness?" Mungo asked unreservedly.

Owein brushed off the indelicacy of Mungo's concern, discerning its innocence. "When I was born, my father decided to establish a new line of kingship, hoping to extinguish our ancestral feuds and restore the Righteous Reign. I cannot impart the name of Bedwas to another until it has been ordained – until I receive the sword of Bedwas – and that cannot happen until the line of Aelhairn has ended." Owein contemplated his words while studying the rustic hardtack. "Until my father passes into the New World." Mungo perked up at the mention of his precious passion, but restrained himself once he apprehended the context. "As it happens," Owein resumed, sighing in his spirit, " Ayla Breaca is said to be a lunatic, addled with the Madness of the Sea. The engagement was a mockery. In any case, Dunragit would hang her, along with all of Tur, before seeing her wed to the son of Urien the Conspirator. All of that, and I've never even met the poor girl. So you see, my father has consigned me to a prison within prisons."

Mungo appeared intensely interested in his partner's narrative, as if his beloved Nana was telling him a story of the Old World. "But how can you be the king if you're not really, you know, a king?" he blurted obliviously.

Owein knew that he should be outraged by Mungo's tactlessness, and yet he found it oddly refreshing. He had grown weary of the false adulation and feeble deference which his subjects invariably expressed; in fact he despised it. "When my father absconded, he left the kingdom in no slight predicament; for though he was absent, he was not known to be deceased. I have acted as king only on his behalf." Owein experienced the pungent mixture of shame and relief that comes from confessing an unbearable secret. For the first time, he was able to let down his laboured facade of self-possession. "His return, and subsequent disappearance, have complicated matters further; but in truth, I am no king at all; only a prince."

"That ain't true, Y'r Highness," Mungo retorted brashly. "You're the King of Righteousness. It said so on the mem'ry stone."

~ **Chapter 29** ~

Gerar was a monument of ignominy. The bleak estuary was once a pillar of trade thanks to its providential supply of sea salt, the benign tides of the Jacinth Sea mixing with the fresh currents of the Mull River to beget pristine crystals of flavour, healing, and preservation. Yet when the Sea retreated with the Saints, the River twas left to fill her marshy pools in sterile contrition. The River's mouth, moreover, had been so distended by the Sea's withdrawal that a flat pan of shallow water now stretched beyond the pale, effectively precluding its use as a harbour. Since the beginning of the Sixth Age, Gerar had been a childless widow, forsaken and forgotten.

It was high noon when the landfarers arrived, and the stillborn ocean was gilded with a cloudless sheen.

"Suppose we didn't plan too well," Mungo opined blithesomely, capering down from his horse. "No chance of finding that star in the middle of the day. Suppose we could use the rest anyhow. You nev'r did take your kip."

Owein gazed out into the lifeless sea as it engorged itself with the river's outflow. It was her Emerald sister which, with the same morbid satisfaction, drank the bitter blood of the Mara. "We cannot linger here," he declared abruptly. "I am now within a day's ride of Wetherstag. That is where I should be – not here, chasing rainbows and squandering precious time. I will not repeat the offense of my father – I will not abandon Rheged in its time of need."

Mungo was strangled with anguish, his face turning as pale as the ocean. "But Sire," he forced out of his constricted throat, hoping to discover that his consternation was unfounded. "The mem'ry stone – it says we need to be here. You can't leave now!"

Perched above his guide, Owein was once again the stern general, concerned only with the burden of his duty and the defence of his country. "The Kingdom stands on a precipice – it may have already fallen for all I know! The Councilmen are either incompetent or seditious. Rheged needs its king!"

"But Sire," Mungo protested, nearly in tears, "if you want to save the Kingdom..."

Owein had dispensed with his prior clemency. "Do not presume to tell me how to save my own kingdom, Mungo Caldbeck!"

Mungo's grief now combined with frustration so that pathetic sobs were stifled by a furrowed scowl. "Well, what about me? We've only got one horse! Am I supposed to go with you to Wetherstag?"

"Yes," Owein replied impassively. "I'm afraid that is our only option. Once we reach Wetherstag I will arrange for you to be escorted back to Watendlath, or wherever you wish to go. Your service to Rheged will be honoured."

"Well, I ain't goin'," Mungo announced, folding his arms and planting his backside on the ground. "You'll have to find the way on your own."

"Gerar has been here since the First Age," Owein averred, his earthward gaze betraying a lack of conviction. "It will still be here, should we return at a more propitious hour."

Mungo shook his head spasmodically, his lips puckered shut. "So be it," Owein responded, turning his eyes to the river. "The route is straightforward enough. Here," he gestured, extracting a satchel of provisions and tossing it down to Mungo. "You will need this more than I. It should last a week if you're prudent." With that, he snapped the reins and set off along the river.

"I'll be wanting that Morag back!" Mungo shouted pitifully, leaping to his feet. "She's me Uncle Frigg's!"

~ Chapter 30 ~

"That's the fifth town we've lost in as many days!" Dunragit rasped through a hoarse throat. For as many days, Dunragit had once again confined himself to the throne room. "Surely we can keep this demoniac at bay, if not send him back into Hell?"

Berlewen Hoel conveyed his explanation with a quiver, as if it terrified him. "Sire, Albion is indeed a man possessed. He stops only to rape, kill, and burn." Hoel paused to collect himself, aghast at his own recountal. "And his movements are ambiguous – he seems to have no strategy, at least none that can be predicted."

Dunragit scratched his bleary eyes with a clenched fist, indicating both exhaustion and exasperation. "Do we yet know if General Uchdryd survived?" he croaked jadedly.

Vicereine Osla responded with her usual directness, though even her aplomb had been thrown off kilter. "Albion rides with Uchdryd's head on a spike. He flaunts it as a banner."

Dunragit rested his heavy head on his heavy arm, which rested on his heavy throne. Yet he promptly rallied, as if he were relieved to be bearing one less burden. "We must attend to the gaping hole that Albion has left in our defences. Keir's forces are weakened, but it is surely a matter of time before Owein sends reinforcements."

"Perhaps not, Sire," Beggerin suggested. "I have received word that Ravenshield has fallen to the Qa." Beggerin waited for the revelation to impress itself before drawing its implication. "That should absorb most of Owein's attention – and most of his forces." Dunragit performed an impulsive double-take, furrowing his eyebrows with tentative interest.

Hoel stepped forward, eager to give his opinion. "We should eject the Qa from Cromlech before they get too comfortable, now that the deed is done. You know what those black-blooded barbarians are like – greedy as pigs and crafty as foxes."

"Cromlech is of no use to us at present," Dunragit grated irritably, now supporting his forehead with outstretched fingers. "In any case, we cannot spare the troops. We must hope that Dahaka stays occupied with Owein, just as Owein stays occupied with Dahaka."

Osla frowned with analytic concentration, laconically voicing her concern. "What then of Albion? He continues to harry the Land unchecked."

Beggerin intervened to prevent the diversion. "Owein may withdraw him to shore up the capital now that Ravenshield lies in the hands of the Qa – perhaps we should wait before committing ourselves to an irreversible course of action. As you said, Sire, we can ill afford to disperse our forces."

Dunragit squinted searchingly at Beggerin, as if reading in the dark. "That wretch Albion has been waiting for this opportunity since he was born," he finally demurred, "all the more so since Urien expelled him from Glaramara. He would not fall back if he was ordered to do so by Elyon Himself." Dunragit's voice modulated to a cagey requiem. "You are correct, however, that we cannot spread ourselves too thinly, for we cannot fortify every town in Durdich. Sooner or later Albion will reach Blencathra and Helvellyn. It must be his own head on that spike if he thinks he can match us there."

Hoel grimaced with outrage. "Sire, with the utmost respect, would you leave Marana to be consumed?"

"What do you propose, Berlewen?" Dunragit snapped back, aggravating his windpipe. "That I let the monster make sport of me as I chase him through the Marches like an angered bull? We'd have better fortune sailing off into the Beryl Sea in the hope of finding the Lost Land. No, we must engage him in our own terms."

Beggerin shifted towards the throne, an oily grin smeared on his face. "May I suggest, Sire, that we consider the situation as an opportunity?"

Dunragit scrutinised the oncomer as if to measure his stature. Hoel, on the other hand, reacted impulsively. "Spare us your tiresome equivocations, Beggerin," he entreated querulously. "Say what you mean – and for the sake of the Land, mean what you say."

Beggerin sniggered at the request before gladly discharging it. "No doubt we are vulnerable, Sire, but Rheged is more vulnerable still. As you so judiciously observed, Keir's forces are depleted. The way to Wetherstag lies open – and I doubt even the City of the Old Fathers can withstand the weight of both Aram and Durdich. Of course, the Qa may not require our assistance..." Again, Beggerin let the bait rest before setting the hook. "But if it is they who take the city, we will lose our claim to its dominion."

Dunragit was now glaring lividly at Beggerin, who duly twitched with confusion. The king continued to bore his eyes into the adviser, as if to crush his crooked back even further into the ground. Seeking reprieve, Beggerin began to speak, but Dunragit interrupted him. "Uchdryd's is not the only head that has recently seceded from its body. Three days ago a riderless horse was sent down Golgotha. The Qa now hold all of Abaddon, of course, so it was they who intercepted the animal. It carried the head of Emrys Morraine."

Hoel tutted with mild regret. "Morraine was a useful traitor. Perhaps it's for the best, though," he gabbled cursorily, "it was never certain where his loyalties truly lay."

"Aye," Dunragit trenchantly affirmed while aiming his sights back at Beggerin, who this time froze like a stunned deer. Eventually the king stood up from his throne and, folding his hands behind his back, began pacing across the dais. "The Qa are evidently worried that we will exploit the distraction of Ravenshield by mounting a surprise attack on Aram. To curry our favour, they appended an informative note to the traitor's head before sending it on to us." Dunragit, mimicking Beggerin's own tactic, left his listener in suspense before executing the coup de grace. "The note claims that Morraine was not the only traitor."

"Lies!" Beggerin spouted venomously, inferring the implication. "Don't you see, Sire, that this is a ploy to foment division in our ranks?"

Dunragit glanced halfway round to the accused, disregarding his appeals. "I do not forget your heroism, Beggerin Achill — your disfigurement is a visible reminder of the sacrifice that the Land requires. For that reason I will spare your life." Haunted once more by the spectre of his duty, Dunragit conducted an internal exorcism before continuing. "In any case, there has been too much talk of disembodied heads today. I am weary of the thought." Dunragit then turned to face the convict. "No, Beggerin, you will die at a ripe old age, after you have spent the rest of your miserable days regretting your crimes as you languish in the Prison of Bashan."

~ Chapter 31 ~

The Mull River, with its source in the Kidron Hills, marked the conventional border between Brambia and Rheged; but since Brambia itself had no official standing, neither did its border. It was Gorsedd Cadell who partitioned the Kingdom, exploiting natural barriers to govern trade and migration – a function which became redundant when, in no small part thanks to Cadell's own government, the movement of goods and people diminished. The Mull, too, had slowed to the point that its motion was nearly indiscernible, and in places it resembled more of a lagoon than a river. For Owein's purposes, however, it provided a convenient guide to the centre of Rheged.

Although his passage was simple to navigate, it was impeded by a head-on clash of boisterous winds. One moment, he was thrust forward by a southwesterly gust; the next, he was rebuffed by a northeasterly gale. The queer sensation that both forces were prevailing at once – that they were simultaneously pushing and pulling, generating a concentrated current of static tension – was enough to perturb even the equanimous Morag, who had to be coerced into compliance by her dizzy master. Amid the invisible friction, both creatures gradually experienced an even more distressing phenomenon – a rapacious thirst, exacerbated by the constant sound of moving water. They were quickly surfeited with the mildewed discharge to the point of nausea; yet they kept drinking, for the thirst would not be quenched.

The Kidron Hills were often seen, but almost always from afar.

Nestled within the outlying purlieus of the capital city, they formed the tacit frame for more significant sights, the ancillary backdrop for more worthwhile destinations. They were even less notable when approached from the south, where their gentle slopes lacked the prominent contours of the northern aspect. Tonight, though, irradiated by star-spangled vaults, their interfolded vales welcomed the King himself. Owein wondered whether the Star of Esa had joined the celestial host, but he dare not look back, choosing instead to suppress his conviction in wilful blindness.

Morag, however, would not be so easily deluded; nor, as she conveyed through obstinate brays and pounding hooves, would she yield to Owein's previous tactic of sheer duress. Despite a lifetime of bearing loads and hauling ploughs in dutiful obedience, she would go not one step further; she would rather defy a king than transgress against Elah Himself. Ultimately, Owein's royal status could not avail him against a considerable disparity in physical strength. Cursing the animal's stubbornness, Owein elected to proceed on foot.

Owein reckoned that he had passed the river's source, for he could no longer see, hear, or taste its indolent trickle. He was relieved to be free from its sarcastic tribute, which only intensified his relentless thirst; yet he mourned the loss of its steady direction. Not for his life would he risk consulting the cosmos; on the contrary, his line of sight became even more earthward as he drifted from hill to hill, glen to glen, slavishly following his feet wherever they would take him.

Owein's introspective wander was interrupted by a shrill bleat, immediately followed by a belligerent choir. Owein turned to behold a host of white wool, glowing in the night light, charging towards him over interwoven undulations. He had not expected to meet anyone or anything until he reached Tabor on the opposite side of the range; and although he was wary of encountering wild animals, the thought of being hunted by a herd of rabid sheep had never crossed his mind. He had evidently trespassed into a restricted territory, a realm not answerable to the kingdoms of men, and would be dealt with accordingly. Flummoxed as to how the herd would engage him, and thus how he would defend himself, he stood transfixed against the oncoming threat.

When the predators had nearly reached their prey, a plangent voice rumbled across the hillside: "Peace!" The sheep immediately obeyed, coming to an abrupt halt as the issuer of the command emerged on the hilltop, towering above his realm with crook in hand. "Fear not," he duly instructed, descending towards Owein.

"I did not mean to intrude," Owein proffered guardedly, cautious not to peer too highly into the sky. "I am destined for Tabor."

"No, you're not," the stranger countered genially, chuckling as he spoke. "This isn't the Way, I'm afraid. That's why the sheep came at you — they knew you were going the wrong way." He extended his hand as he reached Owein, his sheepskin fleece wafting a distinctive bouquet of ripened and digested grass. "I am Feolan Peadar."

"Pleasure to meet you, Feolan Peadar," Owein replied, accepting the gesture but withholding his own name. The unkempt native seemed not to notice the omission.

"These are my sheep," the shepherd avouched proudly as he introduced his flock. "That's Yan and Tan in front," he boasted, gesticulating friskily with his stick. "The brawny ones are Tether, Sether, Mether, and Hether – she's the youngest, Hether, but you couldn't tell her that! Hother and Dother are the ones grazing – always eating, those two! I know this lot better than I know myself."

Owein was unsure whether he had chanced upon a lunatic, or whether he himself had gone mad. "Can you set me on the correct path?"

Feolan shaped an apologetic grimace as he glanced around his nocturnal habitat. "There's no paths in these hills – only a maze of sheep trails. And no shortage of wolves. You'll be better off waiting for daybreak." He let the air settle before stepping towards his flock. "Come," he invited affably, signalling with his crook, "I'm gathering these beasties into a shelter on yon hillside. You can lodge there for the night." Owein was about to decline when Feolan enhanced the offer. "There's plenty of fresh water…"

***

Owein had not anticipated that the refreshment would be served in a trough, nor that he would be compelled to share the offering with a mob of grubby sheep which were apparently ill-disposed to his presence. He seemed to have developed a habit of boarding in the midst of malodorous animals – one which he swore to renounce forthwith. The water, though, was fresh indeed; and for the first time since leaving Gerar, his thirst was mollified.

Feolan was visibly gratified by the reaction of his guest. "Straight out of the spring, that water. Only the best for my sheep."

"Thank you, Feolan," Owein murmured, rolling onto his back. His protracted tiredness, temporarily numbed by the torment of thirst, had suddenly returned. "In the morning, would you be so kind as to show me the way to Tabor?"

Feolan looked up to the heavens as if reminiscing over a fond memory. "Never seen that star before," he commented wistfully, motioning subtly with his crook. "Never seen you before, neither." His gaze returned to the earth as he pronounced his conclusion. "In the morning we'll go to the Terebinth. Then you can be on your Way."

Owein had no desire to trifle himself with detours, not least to some undefined, unheard-of object; but he desired even less to prolong the bizarre evening. "I shall see you in the morning, Feolan Peadar. Thank you again."

"Don't mind the sheep," Feolan advised serenely as he began to leave. "They won't bother you now that they know who you are."

~ Chapter 32 ~

Owein slept a dreamless sleep, in which a mere candle of consciousness was kept aflame. By the time he awoke, he had forgotten that he was ever alive, like a child when he first enters the world. He was immediately overwhelmed by a tsunami of stimulation – the sound of gypsy birds, billing and cooing as they drifted purposely to ocean skies; the smell of earthen air, incarnating what is above and resurrecting what is below; the sight of matron ewes, watching in restful contentedness as they chewed and breathed and lived.

As his eyes adjusted to the spectrum of foreign colours, he noticed Feolan sitting cross-legged among his sheep, his tatty mantle transfiguring him into one of his own. The shaggy shepherd was all that Owein could recall from his past life. "You have slept, my friend," the herdsman initiated emphatically. "You have slept indeed." In his newborn dumbfoundment, Owein had not yet remembered how to speak, nor did he know what to say. "Come, drink," Feolan continued, opening his palm towards the nearby trough, "and then we will go to the Terebinth." Owein, with no reason to contravene the instruction, duly complied.

As they departed from the sheepfold, the steady pendulation of loosening legs resuscitated Owein's mind. He recalled everything – from where he had come and to where he was going. He was ready to cancel the diversion when Feolan intercepted his intention. "Not long now," the shepherd assured him, pointing his loyal staff toward a gap in the hillside, "just over yon saddle". Owein reluctantly acceded. Even if he wished to depart, he had no sense of location or direction. The intermediate landmark would at least afford him a view of the surrounding area so that he could regain his bearings.

Once the view was attained, however, it was the Terebinth that captured Owein's attention. There was nothing particularly exceptional about the tree, which stood alone in the neighbouring dale, nearly lost amid the multitude of wild ryegrass; and yet there was a music about it, a psalm which rustled in the gentle sway of its plentiful leaves and resonated through the silent stillness of its noble trunk. Its roots reached deep, its branches high, to redeem the water of earth and inherit the light of Heaven; it was a child of spirit and a mother of matter, a sentry stationed at the threshold of reality.

Feolan grinned to himself when he observed Owein's enchantment. "It's been here for ages, that tree," he remarked tenderly, evincing a personal affection, "but it keeps growing – slower than anyone could ever notice, but grow it does, surely and steadily. It was once just a wee acorn – then a seedling, then a sapling. Now look at it – a mighty hardwood."

Owein followed his guide down into the cloistered valley and on towards the Terebinth. The dense-aired lowland seemed to lie above the world, overseeing its eternal patterns and transcending its man-made limitations. "This branch has been growing since you were born," Feolan stated calmly, passing his hand over a young limb as if to appreciate its craftsmanship. "All the while you were sleeping, it's been growing. Look," he indicated with happy surprise, delicately handling a cluster of acorns, "it's even begun to bear fruit." Feolan carefully plucked an acorn from the branch before inspecting it scrupulously. "Yes, this is the one," he mumbled to himself delightedly. Jubilant yet heartbroken, like a father commending his daughter to marriage, he gently passed the acorn to Owein. "This is why you are here, my friend."

Not for the first time, Owein wondered if his genial cicerone was moonstruck. Yet in this place – this place outwith any place, yet within every place – somehow he apprehended that the last was always first. He felt, too, that the humble gift contained a kernel of this radical meaning, a germ of this surpassing truth.

Once the treasure had been bequeathed, the shepherd-savant continued his revelation with newfound sternness, his eyes moving from object to subject. "The Kingdom is now in your hand. You must tarry no longer, Owein son of Urien." His crook was once again wielded as a waymarker, this time pointing down the valley's southern corridor. "You must regain your path."

***

Owein had no intention of disputing the shepherd's edict, at least until he reached the valley's entrance. Not only did he lack an alternative bearing by which to resume his journey to Wetherstag, but he was in some way relieved to part company with his peculiar host. To be sure, the herder had exuded a distinctive aura of peace and comfort; but this was counterbalanced by his uncanny aptitude for personal discernment. He felt as if this Feolan Peodar had seen straight into his soul, with all of its shame and doubt. Besides being a prophet, the man was some kind of enchanter; and although his intentions were clearly benign, his methods still galled Owein, who once again found himself resisting the mysterious and the supernatural.

The farther Owein withdrew from the Terebinth, the less its spaceless vitality prevailed. With each step, he felt himself descending to a lower, more restricted level of consciousness, in which he viewed the world from the perspective of himself rather than the richer, more meaningful inverse. It was as if he were stepping back into a mirror which had imprisoned him since birth, allowing him to see out, but not in. Minded again to continue his errant quest, he sought to regain the surrounding heights in order to chart a course to the capital. As he relocated to the valley's edge, however, he encountered a shy, cold beck, trickling softly among the ryegrass. Somehow he recognised the hidden stream; and, though it was not wide enough to bear his reflection, somehow he recognised himself in its quiet waters. He could sense and almost taste its sweet freshness, which reminded him of the deep rest of the sheepfold. Surely this was the same water he had then imbibed; and surely it now flowed within him, revealing the Ancient Way of Dalriada and carrying its holy blessing to a world made new.

As Owein traced the timid stream, it intermittently disappeared and reappeared in the untamed meadow, as if teasing him with a girlish bashfulness; yet when he reached the end of the valley, it suddenly matured into a full-grown river. Owein identified it immediately as the

Mull, now absolved of its former impotence, parading victoriously to its eternal home. He wondered what had come of Morag, whom he had deserted on its lonesome banks – and indeed, what had become of Mungo. The seasons had changed since he first reached Kidron in the late autumn, for it was now undoubtedly spring, the rusty-bronze tinge of drowsy decay replaced by the golden brilliance of raw rebirth. The full length of his dereliction was impossible to determine, but certainly the Acolyte would have returned to his country by now. Owein prayed that his opportunity had not expired; that Esa would still shine in the night sky; that Tur could still be saved.

As he pressed on with urgency and remorse, he found himself being herded by a gentle zephyr, blown to and fro like the catkins that had swayed in the branches of the Terebinth. The childlike wisdom that had blossomed within him testified that this was the Yom of Sukkot – the very Word of Elyon, which no longer contended with its southerly foe, instead returning full-bodied and unbridled toward the Jacinth Sea. *Yes*, he thought to himself. *There is still a Way.*

~ Chapter 33 ~

Owein had not expected to find Mungo in the alluvial colony of Gerar, where they had last shared each other's company, but he was nonetheless disheartened when his assumption was confirmed: amid all the evidence of bygone activity, his trustworthy companion was nowhere to be found. Owein repressed his urge to weep as he parked himself in a deserted salt hut, but the alkaline air thrust its worthless commodity into his face, wringing tears from his eyes as if to make reprisal for its own bereavement. Seeking distraction, he removed Feolan's acorn from his chest pocket to study its features. How could something so humble, so simple, represent the Kingdom, let alone contain it? Mungo, too, was humble and simple; yet he had embodied the Kingdom of the Old Fathers more faithfully, more truly, than had the king himself. Owein wept, more loudly, more bitterly, than he had ever allowed himself to weep.

Night was falling when Owein left the storehouse. The forsaken place was somehow more dignified in the moonlight, its grey wrinkles alchemised into silver filaments. Then Owein remembered – moonlight, starlight...Esa. He mopped the brine from his eyes to behold the Star, still fastened to its position in the night sky though the galaxies had shifted. Possessed by determination, he strode down to the shoreline, where an obsolete pier had been reclaimed by a thicket of mangroves. After reaching the end of the flimsy jetty, he stopped to gaze into the inky sphere of sea and sky, which professed that there was nothing for him on Tur except death and destruction – not for anyone, unless he fulfilled his purpose, the purpose of his father, the purpose of his father's fathers. Uncertain but determined, he stepped down into the saline perdition, the end of which was said to lie in the great hereafter – the world beyond the world, the life after life, the Land of the Shai. At first he could walk unhindered atop the shallow seabed, as if through a puddle; but gradually his feet sank and the water rose until he was wading knee-, then waist-, then shoulder-deep through the brackish ebb, his ceremonial drapery dragging him down into the murky depths.

After miles and hours of gradual descent, he reached a point where either his foothold or his respiration would have to be sacrificed. Keeping his eyes fixed on the celestial beacon, he marched forward, surrendering his moribund body to the nodding tide. He prepared to swim as his head submerged, expecting the seafloor to recede beneath him; but instead, his flailing foot struck firm ground. He clambered onto the protrusion, resisting the impotent pulsations of the ocean swell to take one step, then two, then three, each step reversing his immersion as the bulge revealed itself to be a salient ridge lying inches below the surface. Eventually he was strutting liberally along the invisible highway, which pointed straight toward the Star of Esa.

Owein walked through the night, shivering beneath his sodden garments. His mind recoiled inwards to ignore the chill, the aloneness, the jeopardy of his situation, focusing solely on the next step and the final destination. He recited the epitaph at Bethelah over and over like a mantra, assuring himself that his squelching path led somewhere other than the abyss:

> "Far across waters must he walk
> *Until he reaches solid rock.*"

He found himself thinking once again of Mungo, who had first uttered the line that now buoyed his spirit. He recalled how they had endured similar circumstances together, how Mungo's unflappable company had kept him sane even while challenging his sanity. "Always remember the stories," Mungo had exhorted him. "Sometimes they're all we've got. That's what Nana used to say." Owein reminisced of his own mother, whose escapist storytelling he had long striven to escape. He recalled the lyrics that he had once heard her recount to herself, sometime after Urien had departed on his quest:

> "The bridge, the breach; the door, the key;
> The thread through time, tied together
> In a circle. It ties together
> What is, what was, and what is to be.
> Under the sky, above the sea
> It lies in perfect symmetry.
> It splits the oceans, joins the lands –
> At the edge of worlds, Langstrath stands."

Thanks to his royal schooling, Owein knew the stanza to be an excerpt from the apocryphal Lindisfarne Chronicles – which, like the words of Bethelah, were composed in the characteristic pentameter of the early Sixth Age. 'Langstrath' had always been interpreted as the corridor of holy wind known as the Yom of Matzot, Elai's Whisper, the very wind that carried Gildas and his saints to the holy isle of Iona. In turn, the phrase 'Langstrath stands' had been explained as merely a stylistic device, contrived to accord with poem's rhyme. Perhaps, though, the silty reef on which Owein now stood was the true subject of the familiar fable; perhaps Owein was himself a successor of Gildas Bedwyr.

When sunlight finally superseded moonlight, it was eclipsed by a shape that did not throb with the nauseous movement of the sea, but rather stood still like a star. Owein plodged on excitedly as he attempted to espy the stationary mass, which rested on the horizon directly beneath the spot where Esa had watched the seasons pass. As light came into the world, and the world came to the light, Owein was able to perceive that it was dry land – a rough protuberance of solid rock, jutting up from the very foundations of the earth. He sobbed again, this time with joy, hurling himself wholeheartedly along the final section of the hidden bridge. The island seemed to grow no nearer as he approached it; but then suddenly he was there, on its rugged shores, standing at the edge of worlds.

~ Chapter 34 ~

Owein circuited the island with a mixture of childish fascination and primal desperation. Unless this heap of rock contained something of use, something of significance, it would become his final resting place; and though eternal rest was not without allure, he knew there would be no rest for Rheged if he were to die here. The recession of the seas was evident even on this littoral enclave; for though it was high tide, a wide ribbon of shingle remained dry as bone. It was there, on the windward shore, that Owein discovered a marooned coracle, lying a stone's throw beyond the high watermark. The vessel must have washed up by chance, Owein surmised, for even the languid drift of the Jacinth Sea would be impossible to navigate without sail or scull; yet he detected no rot or decay in its timbered frame. Either it had been miraculously preserved for nearly three ages, or it had been intentionally docked within the month.

Owein scanned the island's perimeter before casting his eyes to the craggy peak which marked the island's apex. If anyone was here, they would be there. The climb required energy which Owein had to borrow from his own constitution; but his investment was rewarded with pools of fresh rainwater and shrubs of wild currants, which he consumed copiously before reposing on a prominent slab. Drawing a deep breath, he surveyed the rolling tides of the Jacinth Sea as they laboured under the midmorning sun, which had nearly dried his tattered outfit. To the north he could observe the faint outline of the Turian coast; to the south, nothing but endless ocean. To be still, to participate in the continuous stillness of the world – here he could indeed rest forever.

Despite his previous assumption, affected as it was by delirium and dread, he now realised that Iona, if it in fact existed, would be located farther to the east. Surely Langstrath would begin in Lanercost, where Gildas Bedwyr began his mission; yet that long-lost port was rumoured to lie in modern-day Durdich, a hundred leagues from his own origin in Gerar. Even if Langstrath was a passage of wind rather than the solid peninsula which Owein had traversed, as per the popular legend, it would have to take a peculiar course indeed to reach the point where Owein now lay. On the other hand, it had been speculated that the contraction of the seas was accompanied by a change in the prevailing winds, and perhaps even a shift in the ocean floor. In any case, who was to say that there were not two entrances to the elusive Long Strait, or even two different manifestations? Owein again caressed the acorn in his front pocket. Mungo would have known.

The heaviness of his legs, eyes, and soul soldered Owein to his seat, but the impulse to complete his quest cleaved him from it. He had followed the Star to this secret land; there must be some purpose for the excursion. He reconnoitred the island's rooftop with a kind of haphazard assiduousness, every now and then turning over a rock or peering over the bluff, searching intensively for he knew not what. His attention had begun to wane when his eye caught a glare emanating from the island's pinnacle rock, which towered over the sea like a refuge in the sky. He cut a beeline across the intervening boulder field, using what little energy he had left to scramble over the remains of primeval eruptions.

The summit itself was a challenge to scale, but the unexpected reward was worthy of the effort: a glorious broadsword standing upright, its shaft of silver steel radiating shafts of golden light, the pearls in its pommel glowing whiter than white. The blade's cruciform spanned from the North to the South, its crossguard from the East to the West; its extremities embraced Heaven and earth, its intersection made them one. As Owein neared the weapon, he noticed that it stemmed from the stone as if it had germinated there organically, or as if it had been forged in situ by a tremendous bolt of lightning; for there was no cleavage in its petrified pedestal to indicate any extraneous insertion. Hesitantly, he extracted the celestial sword from its terrestrial scabbard; it slid through the rock as if through water. As he raised the sunlit blade to his sunburnt face, he beheld an engraving across its surface: "*The Edge of Worlds*". His heart fluttered and then seemed to stop altogether as he beheld the single name on the opposite side, composed in bold, august letters: "*Langstrath*".

~ Chapter 35 ~

Owein stood atop the island's spire with outstretched arms, feeling the ocean air direct him like a weather vane. The wind had changed since he harvested the sword: previously a northerly breeze, it now rushed back to the mainland as if to herd him home. Indeed, if there was something of his companion Mungo in the stubborn faith of his outward journey, and something of his mother, there was something of the shepherd Feolan in the caring authority of this providential gale, and something of his father. With sword in hand, Owein knew that he could not return to the continent the way he had come; for he was now Bedwas Owein, King of Rheged, and it was now his mission to liberate Tur. Gildas had sailed to Iona to preserve the Ancient Way; now, Owein would restore it. That was the Prophecy of Enoch, which his mother had sung to him as a child and which his father had assigned to him as a man.

There was no sheath for the lusty blade, for it had been born of water and spirit – an immaculate conception. Indeed, it seemed that no sheath could contain it, for it was the Edge of Worlds; it would sever any division, block any obstacle, defeat any death. Langstrath must be grasped – and grasped firmly, for it seemed longer, wider, and heavier than any sword wrought by man. Owein's own body, however, would still require a vessel if he was to brave the open seas. Fate had prepared one for him; and though the coracle which Owein had discovered upon arrival was feeble and primitive, Owein knew that its quality would not determine the success of his voyage.

After descending to the island's lower skirt – no mean feat while clutching a two-handed hilt – Owein dragged the coracle to the place where the water met the land. He ventured one final gaze around the island – a harbour of dreams, a stepping stone of destiny, a halfway house between this life and the next. As he manoeuvred the craft into the water and climbed inside, clutching Langstrath to his chest, it felt as if he was interring himself in his own grave; yet he was content, for, like his forefathers, he would be buried a king, with sword in hand and peace at heart.

~ Chapter 36 ~

In contrast to its previously subdued pulsations, the tide now palpitated convulsively as the lovelorn sea raced to embrace the war-torn land, wailing with its dirge and dancing to its chorus. Owein rolled, pitched, and yawed without sense of duration or direction, his frail coracle straining under the redemption of time and space. Over time, and over space, his consciousness turned utterly inwards, shrinking into innumerable layers of concentric selfhood. The condition was similar to what he had experienced in Feolan's sheepfold, except that this time he dreamed. This time, moreover, he delved so deeply into his own being that he escaped it; he reached the essence of his substance, and there found life itself, composed only of life itself. The contents of the dream, therefore, he could not tell, not even to himself; for it could only exist as dream. In truth, it was not so much what he saw as how he saw it. It was a way of seeing, a way of being; it was the Ancient Way.

His craft was beached when he awoke; but his head still wrenched and lurched with the motion of the sea, leaping to and fro like a newborn lamb celebrating newfound life. His mind was muddled save a few lines of scripture, which echoed faintly but emphatically in the many mansions of his soul. Whether he had recalled the verse from a dormant corner of his memory, or whether they had been revealed to him in the waking darkness of his dream, it made no difference; indeed, he sensed that there was no difference, for he had seen the light which is before all light, the light by which light is seen, the light which enlightens all people and illuminates all things.

As he breached the layer of salt which had caked over his eyes, his first sight upon coming into the world was not the distant welkin that he expected, lying supine as he was; instead, he was confronted by a freckle-faced sprite peering into the coracle with an open-mouthed smile. "Sire!" the red-haired fellow exclaimed with familiar vivacity. "Y're here! Y're finally here!"

Owein blinked deliberately a few times, adjusting to his unfamiliar awareness and assuring himself that he was not still dreaming. His wide-eyed counterpart blinked back at him. It was Mungo.

~ Chapter 37 ~

Urien was anchored to an arid underworld, confined to its motionless walls with the eternal torment of a light that would never reveal itself; yet he felt naked on a wet and windy night, with nothing on which to anchor his hope. He sat listlessly and absently, waiting for something but refusing to think about anything.

Urien was stirred by the sound of footsteps. His spirits were suddenly quickened, stricken with the fever of battle – the perspiration, the respiration, the palpitation; the tightening of muscles and the clenching of teeth; the instinct to kill and live. The light, too, seemed to be intensifying, as if its source were drawing nearer. He sprung to his feet and brandished Trusmadoor, the ancient emblem of the Doves of Shekinah unveiled by the approaching light. The Keepers were coming to claim their prey – perhaps their first since the Third Age. He would make a stand – doubtless his last until the End of Ages.

Urien was paralysed by the light when it finally emerged. The force was not only blindingly bright; it was also deafeningly loud and unbearably heavy, as if its power was unfettered by the world's parameters, as if its matter was more elementary than the world itself. Indeed, the walls seemed to recede at its presence, the very fabric of existence bulging at the seams. Urien felt as if his soul was being eviscerated by the flood of energy which submerged his body.

By the time he recovered, he found himself lying prostrate, not in a ghostly cage, but in a glorious court, with a floor of diaphanous alabaster that seemed to swell and give with the motion of the sea. In its centre was an empyreal being, human in form but clothed in a peculiar light – the prism of Dalriada, which took the form not of an arc, but of a complete sphere, defining reality in never-ending revolutions. Urien could see that the luminous being was one of the Shai, a kinsman of the Priest who had appeared to him while he dreamt in Gwydir's cave. Yet this time Urien was awake, and the presence of the heavenly host was more than his senses could bear. Indeed, Urien imagined that his perception was only possible because he had died, or at least was in a place of death.

When the being spoke, it was as if he was projecting the heat, light, and sound of a raging fire.

"Uryn, son of Eirnyn, son of Uthra, arise!"

The thunderous voice crushed Urien into the ground, as if he were being addressed by Elyon Himself; yet he found himself standing erect, as if it was impossible for the command to be violated.

"Who are you?" Urien cried in terror, discerning that his very life-force was at the mercy of the awesome stranger.

"I am Melchizedek of Shailoh," the being replied, the earth quaking at the eruption of his voice. "I am here to restore your path, Uryn Elaha." Each time the Priest spoke, it seemed an age before the reverberations subsided.

"Why did you not reveal yourself when I pursued you?" Urien asked timidly, dumbfounded by the sheer power of his counterpart yet instinctively distrustful given his still-raw experience of deception.

"You cannot approach the Light," the Priest averred, "but it can approach you; and it will, if you seek it."

Urien's doubts suddenly vanished as the Priest's identity became clear. "You are the Priest who founded the Spring of Seeing."

"Yes," Melchizedek confirmed, "at long last, the Spring has been restored; for you have brought the Water of Dalriada."

Although Urien was initially nonplussed by this temporal paradox, its pronouncement seemed to unblock the spring within him, which not only allayed his lack of comprehension but also quenched his torturous thirst. The Priest's appearance then became less intimidating, commensurate to the form of the old man in the cave.

"Come, let us sit together," the Priest invited as he turned an open palm towards a kingly table, set with a luscious cornucopia of autumn harvest, "for Elai has made you clean."

~ Chapter 38 ~

Owein had arisen from his seaborn casket hungry, thirsty, and weary, yet full of a new life which seemed to rebirth itself in every new moment. He understood now why his father had returned to Rheged a different man; for he, too, was new, and was ever being made new.

Mungo was also different. Most noticeably, he was older: the patchy down that used to dapple his rounded cheeks had ripened into a dense coating of ginger bristles; and his frame, though still wiry, had expanded such that he was now level with his fellow pilgrim. At the same time, Owein felt that it was himself who had grown to reach the other's stature; for Mungo had all along possessed the regenerated awareness that Owein had only just acquired. It was a mature childlikeness, absorbing every moment as it if it were the first; an openness to wholeness, relinquishing the sin of judgement and distinction; a desire to delve deeper into the miraculous mystery of existence, knowing that the bottom will never be reached.

The two had embraced with words beyond words, laughing through tears until the rapture came back down to earth. Each was so bursting with questions and answers that they knew not where to begin; and yet the most burning question had already been answered, for they were both alive. They had broken their fast in holy communion, weltering in the ripples of elation, and now sat by the dwindling fire on which Mungo had broiled their meal of freshly caught fish.

"Is that the sword of Bedwas?" Mungo asked reverently, referring to the object which Owein had yet to release from his grasp. His countrified drawl had not changed, yet his enunciation was less skittish.

"Yes," Owein replied gravely as he rotated the broadsword in his hand, its dual edges glinting formidably in the morning sun. The ramifications of this simple confirmation were weighty, like the sword itself – a cause for celebration but also sobriety.

Owein looked back out to the sea, the lacuna of his soul and the antechamber of his reincarnation. "Where are we, Mungo?"

Mungo grinned, his interest piqued by the query. "Volume Seven, I reckon. I thought we were only in Volume Six, but seeing as how you've already got the sword, we must be in Seven already. It depends on which manuscript you go by, of course – if you count all of Myrddin's addendums, we might well be in Volume Twelve, but most of those have been lost for ages."

Owein looked at once bemused and amused, cherishing the familiarly effusive soliloquy. With chummy exaggeration, he asked, "What in Heaven and earth, and all that is in between, *are you talking about*, Mungo?"

"The Lindisfarne Chronicles, of course!" Mungo warbled, successfully ruffled by Owein's gibe. "See, look," he implored, producing a pocketbook from his rucksack and riffling through its tattered pages. His eyes widened with childlike enchantment when he located the salient passage, which he immediately proceeded to read:

"'The righteous king will come ashore

Where Gildas sailed, in his hand the dagg'r

That crosses wat'rs to restore

The inn'r and the out'r, the early and the latt'r.'

"See?" Mungo urged, thrusting the Book at Owein. "That's how I knew to find you here!" His demeanour then dampened slightly, as if he had recalled some intractable frustration. "Only it doesn't say what happens next – there's sort of a gap before Volume Eight. I think some of Myrddin's addendums tried to fill it in, but I couldn't find them anywhere."

Reminded of his own vexation, Owein stared into the final embers of the dying fire as he replied with solemn bluntness. "Only a few copies survived after Lindisfarne was dissolved, along with the rest of the monasteries." To distract himself from an onrush of resentment, he purposed to survey the sandy coast, but detected little save the remnants of a few dilapidated fishermen's shacks bowing and swaying in the still-strong wind, which forced the dynamic chaos of the Jacinth Sea against the static order of the Turian continent to reenact the mystery of creation. "So this is Lanercost," he murmured pensively before peering back into the smouldering coals, letting his thoughts run their course.

"Mungo," he declared in the fullness of time. His tone was more buoyant, as if he had arrested his indignation and subjected it to a tribunal of hope. "I know what happens next."

~ Chapter 39 ~

"I wonder if you might indulge my curiosity, Melchizedek of Shailoh, by disclosing what became of the Keepers of Shur." Urien was too stupefied to eat in the presence of the Priest, who, having himself supped like a king, was idly scraping out the flesh of a pomegranate rind. "I have yet to encounter any of the heathens," Urien continued, "and yet their witchcraft lingers in this defiled place."

Melchizedek held his spoon upright on the table as if to examine it. Urien could perceive his own reflection in its convex surface as the Priest responded. "You are mistaken, Uryn Elaha. This land is no longer defiled, and no longer does the wickedness of its Keepers abide; for the Water of Dalriada has cleansed it." The Priest inverted the spoon to reveal its concave face, turning Urien's reflection upside down. "But there is always a choice not to see what exists, or to see what does not exist." Melchizedek held the spoon in place for a moment before resuming his leisurely craft, his tone becoming less sombre. "The desert has a way of drawing out what is already in you – your thoughts, fears, and desires, as well as the grace that you carry."

Melchizedek proceeded to tell of a small company of Keepers who had repented of their iniquities. Freed from their former bondage, they set sail across the Amethyst Sea with nothing but the Yom of Shavuot to determine their destination. The Breath of Elai carried their message to distant worlds, lost Some forgotten since the mortification of the seas, when the Shai themselves had left the shores of Tur. Many, however, had refused to renounce their maleficent ways, electing separation over reconciliation, condemnation over absolution, destruction over restoration.

"Yet hope remains," Melchizedek affirmed, letting his voice drop into a deep, soothing hum. Having played with the spoon for most of his discourse, he now set it down on the table, carefully aligning it with his plate. "Hope remains, Uryn son of Eirnyn, King of Peace, for you have returned from your exile. Now you must find the Cornerstone and return it to the Crown of Shainor."

Urien understood the Priest's exhortation in his gut, in his bowels, in his most inward parts – the parts of him which had already lived a thousand lives, which had already gained the wisdom of the ages. Yet his mind's eye, for all its newfound capacity, was unable to grasp it. Shainor was the mythical Mountain of Mist – the mountain which lay in the long-lost land of Shailana, the mountain too high for even the Shai to ascend. Some said that its height was infinite; others that it reached into Elana, the Highest Heaven, the very House of Elyon. At its summit was said to be a lake: the Crown of Shainor. The lands of the world were the jewels in the Crown of Shainor, which contained the entire world in its holy depths. According to some, Elyon removed each jewel, one at a time, and gave it to the Shai to be cut into a perfect shape, with perfect symmetry. Tur, it was said, was now being perfected, and would one day be returned to the Crown as the Diadem – the most precious jewel of all. Some said that it was already being carried by the Shai up the Mountain of Mist. They would ascend for time eternal, always reaching higher, and higher, and higher.

This much Urien understood. Yet Melchizedek had mentioned the Cornerstone, not the Diadem. The Cornerstone, it was said, had been hewn from the Heart of Shainor by the Shai and entrusted by the Shai to the Old Fathers of Rheged, granting them a Priestly blessing to continue the Ancient Way of Dalriada. When the Old Kingdom fell and the Shai departed, the Cornerstone was lost. Some said that the Shai had brought it back to Shailana, keeping it in the holy city of Shailoh; others that they had cast it into the depths of the sea, where it would rest until the curse had ended; others that they had left it somewhere in Golgotha, the narrow passageway which divided the three kingdoms. Those who dreamt of the New World imagined that one day the Cornerstone would be found and the Ancient Way restored.

The myth of the Cornerstone derived from Anathoth, the ancient monastery where the great bards of the Old Kingdom penned such scriptures as the Ula and the Una, the mystical genealogies of the Shai. It was said that Anathoth was once an island until the seas receded; now it lay abandoned at the end of the An Pensinsula, which separated the Jacinth and the Topaz seas. The legend of the Diadem, on the other hand, originated in the monastery of Lindisfarne – a source of parallel, if not rival texts, including eight volumes of the Lindisfarne Chronicles which contained the most extensive description of the Diadem myth. The location of Lindisfarne remained a mystery: some said that it lay on the Isle of Tiree and was consumed by the Great Fire of Gorsedd Cadell; others that it could be found somewhere in the land of Durdich, at the top of one its many mountains or in the middle of one if its many lakes; still others that it was a fiction, the Chronicles a counterfeit.

Urien now wondered whether the two legends, though never mentioned together, were in fact two aspects of the same, eternal truth. Sensing that his questions would be answered in the fullness of time, he redirected the conversation to the Priest's recountal. "If your mission was completed, Melchizedek of Shailoh, why then do you still tarry here?"

"My mission was not completed," Melchizedek answered, sitting up from his reclined position, "for the King of Peace had lost his way. I remained to ensure that the Ancient Way was not lost."

Urien now wondered if the Priest who sat before him was the same being he had encountered in the Ghelt. Again his mind was clouded; he could not picture the face of the woodsman, whom he had only ever seen from afar and in a dream. Nor could he fathom the sequence of events which Melchizedek described; though, again, he knew that the words were true.

"Yet it must be four ages since the Keepers departed," Urien reasoned aloud. "I have not sojourned in Shur for a week."

"The mirror of the wilderness conceals as much as it reveals," Melchizedek replied, opening his arms as if to remind Urien of his surroundings. "You have squandered much time in the desert, Uryn Elaha; but do not despair, for your years of slumber have been redeemed."

~ **Chapter 40** ~

After sharing apologies and forgiveness, memories and stories, laughter and tears, the duo set off the next day with nothing but a name as their destination. Mungo had located Lanercost by piecing together old maps and enhancing them with clues from his storybooks and grandmother's tales; but now that they found themselves deep in Durdian territory, that method would no longer avail them. The problem was not that Durdich was uncharted, but rather that Durdish names had been lost after Cadell abolished the provincial dialects, decreeing the King's Tongue to be the only lawful language. Of maps there were plenty, but none of them would include the name 'Crummock', save any that had somehow escaped the purge.

"If you aim for the centre, you're bound to hit something," Owein submitted on their otherwise silent march, mimicking the folksy cheer that Mungo usually exhibited. "That's what my bow-master used to tell me as a boy. I bet we'll find Crummock if we employ the same tactic." Discerning that his partner's distress had not been assuaged, Owein continued his whimsical anecdote. "I was never any good with a bow — but give me a sword," he blabbed facetiously, swinging Langstrath dramatically through the air, "and I wager I could have won the Battle of Brackentrod single-handed. Would've needed two hands to wield this terror, mind you."

Mungo cringed at Owein's buffoonery. "Tell me what's troubling you, Mungo," Owein pleaded, noting the strange truth that their temperaments had been swapped.

"It's this place," Mungo replied achingly. "It's so sad – and so angry. There's been so much hurt here, so much wrong. Don't you feel it?"

Owein realised that his renewed acuity had been blunted as he travelled inland, as if the journey was retracing the diminishment of a stranded world which had long forgotten what lay beyond the sea. He recalled his diversion to Kidron – the way he had subjected himself to a spiritual drought by defying the sign of Esa. That sign had called him to the way of Gildas Bedwyr, which offered the last hope that Tur would one day be reunited with eternity.

"You have to pray," Mungo advised caringly. "That's why you don't feel it – 'cause you haven't prayed. And if you don't feel it – if you don't know it's there – you won't do nothin' about it. So you have to say the prayers every day, all the time. Here," he urged, offering a dainty psalter from his rucksack. "I know them all anyway." Owein accepted the gift in his spare hand and thanked the giver with a heartfelt smile. "Just make sure you hold on to it as firmly as that sword," Mungo entreated with a reciprocal grin.

Three gifts had been bestowed on Owein: a sword, a book, and an acorn. The sword required at least one hand to be carried, and Mungo's instruction obliged him to reserve the other for the Book. The acorn, though, was his first gift, and Feolan had told him that to hold it was to hold the Kingdom. For now, it would have to remain in his pocket.

~ Chapter 41 ~

Urien had managed to reach the border of Aram unnoticed. His tortuous march across the countryside, while considerably more protracted than a mounted traverse, had concealed his passage from all but the birds of the air and the beasts of the field. After reaching the Clovenstone, the lonesome landmark which signified the gateway to Shur and the end of the world, he had passed through the vast woodland of the Fife and crossed the King's Road between the hills of Duddon and Gilsland. From there he made straight for the Turquoise Sea, avoiding the Rhiellian Belt of Coll, Mallaig, and Tobermory. The final stretch across the peat hags of the Hawes had drained his time and energy, every step representing a problem to be solved and an enemy to be vanquished, each taking him backwards or sideways, up or down, but rarely forward.

He had expected to encounter a Rhegish outpost at the border, but found that the camp had been abandoned – evidently in a rush, for the tents had not been dismantled, nor the storehouse emptied. The remnants were welcome comforts, but Urien was distraught. What peril had come to Coira, his wife, and Bedwas, his son, whom he had himself abandoned? What had become of the Kingdom, the crumbling remnants of which he had left them to rule?

Fortuitous though his arrival had been, he had reached a dead end. Dead ahead stood the impregnable Mountains of Abaddon, whose perils could only be eluded by passing through Golgotha – the triad of sheer defiles which divided the dominions of Tur. That road lay miles to the south and was guarded continuously by all three kingdoms, which used it as a dump for sewage, bodies, and virtue. Urien looked across to the Olivine Sea, and beyond it to the Onyx. According to the storytellers, the main road into Aram had once tracked the base of the cliffs, but had long since been engulfed by the accursed depths to form an impassable reef. In his prior scepticism, Urien had noted with contempt that the putative rising of the water contradicted the primary legend, in which the seas were supposed to have receded. He knew, though, that the apocryphal passage was now his only hope for entering the Black Country, and thus he knew that his only hope was for the seas to change, for the curse to be lifted and the blessing restored. This, he had come to realise, was the purpose to which his son had been called.

~ Chapter 42 ~

The terrain had become mountainous – treacherous but marvellous. Calcified peaks and fractured ridges formed a scabrous skeleton, emerging from its glacial grave like some undead behemoth. Owein and Mungo avoided the hardy crofts and townships that speckled the glens below, for both of their accents would invite suspicion, if not hostility, among a people whose sufferance for interlopers had long since expired. As they espied the vast archipelago of lakes that wove itself through the sinews of the country's flesh, the foreigners began to realise that they would eventually need to solicit directions; yet, deferring that unfavourable task to a last resort, they persisted along the snowcapped spine in the hope that their objective would be revealed some other way.

The pair had made meagre headway when they were engulfed by a suspended rain, which lingered uncannily as if to ensnare any hapless passers-by in its claggy web.

"We're in the clouds, I reckon," Mungo hollered invisibly through the gossamer mist. "If I was bein' honest, I'd say they're prettier from the outside."

"Aye," Owein hooted back. "We'll need to descend before it gets any worse, lest we fall to our deaths."

Mungo's response emerged unequivocally through the ether. "Righty-ho!"

After scrambling to the next depression, they identified a narrow slope of scree to use for their descent. Though its safety could not be divined through the vaporous veil, the alternative was to ascend into further blindness, with equally uncertain conclusions. As they falteringly sacrificed the firmness of the ridge, the steep pile of debris shifted fitfully under their weight, each step triggering a miniature avalanche of slate and soil. Eventually the mountaineers resorted to sliding on their backsides – an exercise which even Owein found himself enjoying, though Mungo expressed his entertainment more vocally.

The mist began to clear as they stumbled down the mountainside, leaving the holy secrets of the over-world to be revealed in another life. They were half-way to the bottom when Urien spied the lake – a deep-blue basin of fells and falls, collecting the tears of the land to soothe the wounded and preserve the dead as they awaited their vindication. He recognised it immediately though he had never before beheld it, for it awakened a memory that he had not yet lived – a memory from his father's quest, which he had inherited as his kingly privilege and his saintly burden. He clutched his sword with jealousy.

"What is it, Sire?" Mungo asked, observing Owein's fixation. "What do you see?"

"Crummock," answered Owein, keeping his eyes locked on the destination. Uncharacteristically, Mungo required no further information: he looked once to the lake, then back to the King, and that was enough.

They made their way down the mountain in concentrated silence, the temptation to view their objective constantly distracting them from the task of reaching it. To Owein, the raucous sound of cascading stones seemed almost impertinent, for he sensed that his destiny was entwined with his destination. Although Mungo shared the presentiment, he exhibited no inhibition in his approach; on the contrary, his nonchalance multiplied as their path unfolded. His concern lay with Owein, who, he noticed, had recently stowed the Book, using his free hand to negotiate the descent.

As they reached the lakeside, the hush of the air became conspicuous, perturbing even, like a taut bow poised for release, as if fate had paused its eternally intricate convolutions to receive a new mandate. The surface of the lake was crystal in its calmness and clarity, revealing the earthly bowl beneath and reflecting the heavenly dome above in a seamless marriage of water and air. Even the conclave of presiding mountains, which had stood still since the birth of the world, seemed to stand yet stiller, as if they had tarried into old age to arbitrate this single moment. The visitors, too, stood still, paralysed by the weight of the moment.

"The Book," said Mungo in what for him was a whisper. Even he was wary of disturbing the silence. "The Book will tell us what happens next."

Owein nodded reverentially, the gesture resembling a partial bow. Delicately, as if handling a newborn child, he unsheathed the Chronicles from his pack and navigated to Volume Seven. He knew not what to seek, but all doubt was removed once he found the salient passage. Owein duly began to read it aloud in the same muted tone as Mungo:

> "Cross the bridges, pardon the crimes,
>
> Which were condemned in evil times.
>
> Repair the walls, allay the tears,
>
> Which have been shed for countless years.
>
> Open the gates, breach the cages,
>
> Which are still sealed, though pass the ages."

Without intermission, Mungo continued the liturgy from memory:

> "Sow the seed, forgive the treason,
>
> For it is nigh the fruitful season.
>
> Circle the compass, straighten its ways,
>
> To make them as in ancient days.
>
> Cross the rivers, all of them four
>
> And bless the vessel in which they pour."

Owein looked at him curiously, unable to locate the lines in the Book. "One of Myrddin's addendums," Mungo explained with an impish grin.

Nodding once more, this time more affirmatively, Owein indicated that he had reached a decision. With a declaration of "So be it," he thrust Langstrath into the ground, its unearthly blade parting the earth with trenchant facility. Mungo could not discern the motivation for the act – an ambiguity which was only compounded by what Owein said next: "Here shall we begin, and here shall it end. At the edge of worlds,

Langstrath stands."

~ Chapter 43 ~

The world flexed with every step, straining beyond its limits in every direction. Though he was as wide-eyed as ever, Mungo was somewhat less loud-mouthed, for he perceived the static storm in Owein's eyes – the same storm that raged in the world around them.

"Four rivers flow into this lake," Owein explained as he led the excursion, anticipating Mungo's interest. "They are the rivers of Shainor. We must cross each of them. This was my father's burden, and now it is mine."

In one telling of the Shainor myth, all the lands of the world were once one, with the Mountain of Mist in the centre. The Four Rivers carried the holy water of Elyon from the Crown of Shainor to the corners of the One Land of Alba, giving life to all the world; Shainor was the place where life begins and never ends. The men of learning speculated that Tur could indeed have been part of a larger continent at some time in the distant past, and that the supposed marring of the seas referred to a geological rift which separated Tur from its mother land. Shailana was thus an actual place, somewhere across the sea or else submerged in its depths, not the magic realm of lore. Others interpreted the tale as mere fable: Shailana was a spiritual world beyond the reach of the physical, a world above our own, or beyond it, but not within it or among it. Yet there were those who saw the world in a different way. They believed that Shainor could not be found by looking in any one place; and yet it was real, it was here, and it continued to renew the waters of Tur as a remnant of the early blessing and a promise of the latter.

Mungo still did not understand why Owein had left Langstrath behind. Although the king had revealed the name of the lake, he had not divulged the verse that had entered his mind during his watery slumber, which continued to haunt him and taunt him: "After three days in the wooden stomach / The king will go the lake called *Crummock*. / In its blessed depths must his kingship drown / If the kingdom is to reclaim the crown." Owein had scoured the Chronicles for the scripture, staying awake each night after Mungo retired to read by the embers of the fire and then stashing the volume to avoid Mungo's curiosity. He knew the task to be futile, for Mungo would have already recognised the name of the lake had the verse been included in the text, to which its original owner had fastidiously fastened his collection of notes and addendums. Perhaps the lines were contained in one of the lost manuscripts, but Owein knew that it mattered not – only he could write his fate, along with that of Tur.

And so Bedwas Owein, son of Aelhairn Urien, son of Aelhairn Eirnin, walked in the way of pilgrimage.

The eastern shoreline was free and open, and the first river was reached before long. It was as ephemeral and eternal as the sunrise and the springtime – the first beginning, which emerges swiftly from the void like the dawn, once and always. And so the East River was crossed.

Sunwise, they continued to the southern branch. Its waters were fair, though never seen; dulcet, though never heard; sweet, though never tasted. For its midday light was unapproachable by what is not light, its midsummer life unfathomable by what is not life. And so the South River was crossed.

The western limb was evanescent and unsettled, an alienation of nature from its nature, a withdrawal of things into themselves. The lungs emptied, the pulse stopped, the eyes shut; light and life fell to dusk and dust. Yet what was buried was planted; and thus futility was fertility. And so the West River was crossed.

The final chapter was not the last, though it was reached in the dead of night, the dead of winter. It flooded the world, and was turned to blood; but the blood made the world alive again. So the law was love and the life was light; and so the North River was crossed.

Then Owein beheld the cross of Langstrath, shining in the morning sun, glistening with the morning dew, breaking through the morning mist. Its pearl-encrusted pommel rested on the blade like a crown, his crown. His hands chafed with emptiness, and he hastened to his birthright, to reclaim it. Mungo, who had been delegated the Book, trailed tentatively.

Owein stood over the sword, remembering the sense of majesty that had surged through him when he first grasped it. His father and his father's fathers had been Kings of Rheged, Protectors of the Realm, Rhegedons of Wetherstag. He would not abdicate his royal duty, for he was Bedwas Owein, and this was his sword. Mungo watched aghast as the heir apparent seized his heritage with truculent zeal, turning the blade up towards the sky and revelling in its manifest glory.

Owein strode to the shoreline with religious deliberation, dwelling on each rhythmic step as if to conduct his own coronation. There he tarried; for in the limpid mirror he descried himself, proud and puissant, confronting ages of shame for himself, his line, and his kingdom. Mungo could not suppress a cry of horror as the imminent king proceeded to swing the sceptre around his head and, releasing it from his strong hold, heaved it toward his enemy's stronghold with his own cry of anguish. The face of the water and the face in the water, both undisturbed since time forgotten, were shattered.

Owein remained standing at the edge of worlds, watching the point at which Langstrath had been injected and from which the lake now pulsated. He had transfused himself from the land in the heart of sea to the sea in the heart of the land, so that all could be one and one could be all. As fluttering waves became throbbing ripples, horizontal stability and vertical symmetry were gradually restored. A cloudless, nectarous rain then fell from above, meeting the water below with innumerable embraces of reunion. Reclining his head to the gracious sky, Owein witnessed at last what his father had attested at first – the rainbow of Dalriada, now arched victoriously from the ends of the earth to the beginnings of Heaven.

~ Chapter 44 ~

For weeks, Urien had been lodged a bowshot from the cliff sides of Abaddon, watching the sea slosh and crash against the rock like a suicidal siege. It was Hanavi – the yearly Time of High Water, which was due to last for another month. Half of Aram would be underwater, the population having retreated to Pashador, Sychar, and other inland townships to see out the inundation. This morning, though, was different. Though the darkness of the night still reigned, Urien noticed that the continual yet fitful sound of water breaking over rock, which echoed in his mind like a traumatic mantra, was absent. He stumbled to the shoreline, squinting to view the place where stone and ocean met.

The black mountains enshrouded the rising sun, which nonetheless filled the sky with a fiery light; it was as if the volcanoes of Abaddon, dormant since the Second Age, were once again erupting. In the growing glow, Urien could discern that the tide had fallen overnight to reveal the bottom of the precipice, skirted by a thin strip of dry land; indeed, the spectacle of beached mullets and seabed kelp indicated that it had fallen faster and lower than ever before. Urien rejoiced – because not the impossible, but rather the inevitable, had betided. Owein had accomplished his task.

Though the byway was reached with ease, its traversal proved more complicated. Steep in places, sharp in others, and everywhere slimmer than his frame, it was no highway. Urien was reminded of his journey to Gwydir's cave – equally precarious yet equally imperative. He sidled onwards, contemplating the mission which Melchizedek had set before him: to retrieve the Cornerstone and return it to the crown of Shainor.

Urien reached Aram the next morning. The Land was truly Black — a spoiled heap of petrified lava riddled with pits and pools, the most prominent forming a network of open-air hovels. The cave dwellings were designed to endure until Yanavi, the Time of Low Water. It was then that the fisherman and mollusc-pickers would return in force, hoping that their families would survive the season as the country degenerated into a septic sewer, a stagnant oasis for diseases to feed and breed. This time, the sea had declined too quickly for them to react, but Urien knew it would only be a matter of time. Scanning the shoreline for its most protuberant point, he singled out a horned peninsula which cut into the retreating sea like a sword.

He reached the headland in the final remnants of the day, as the moon had already taken up its watch. The ocean seemed more vibrant in the twilight, more awake. Somewhere across its unfathomable depths and unreachable breadths lay Qahal, the Heartland, evacuated by its people long ago as it sank into myth. Urien's heart, too, was homeless, yearning for a home which he had never known. He wondered now what lay beyond Tur, the Onyx Sea, and even Qahal — what places would the displaced have found had they cast their sails to the horizon beyond? Would they have sailed for all eternity, or would they have reached the Eternal Land? There could be no end, he thought, for such would be more unthinkable than endlessness.

Urien unloaded his knapsack. His real burden, though, was girded to his waist: Trusmadoor, the Blade of Ages, and now the price of peace, the ransom of reunion, the dowry paid by Heaven on earth's behalf. As he unsheathed the sword, it mirrored the argent tide as if it, too, belonged to the night, this night. The Doves of Shekinah, which once nested on either side of its medial ridge, fluttered restlessly as they reflected the motion of the waves, yearning to make their final journey into immortality.

Urien laid the sword down between the waves. With the first wave, the weapon scraped along the rocky shore, its crown-shaped pommel dragging behind as if to resist the end of the age. With the second wave, it was gone. The tide would carry the sword until it was laid to rest on the ocean floor – until, perhaps, the ocean floor became dry land, and it was once again revealed to a King of Rheged. Urien felt a sea change in his psyche, as if a yoke had been lifted from his neck, the debt of recuperation which he had continually deferred over the past months suddenly coming due. The ground being too spiky to recline, he sat himself against a nearby tumulus, rested his head on his chest, and fell asleep.

He awoke to the twitter of a flock of starlings, which coalesced before him into a living cloud, amorphous yet intricately orchestrated. He waited until the migratory murmuration had faded into the distance, its garbled symphony into silence, before rising to his feet. The tide had fallen further since the night before, but had evidently settled; and though it had lost none of its vitality, it now mingled with the light of the sun. At once, Urien recognised the overflowing grace of Dalriada, which he had first witnessed in the wildwood of the Ghelt and which he had then carried to the wilderness of Shur. He fell to his knees in exultation, ignoring the spiny tridents which cut into his flesh. The curse of the sea had been abolished; the promise of the Priestly blessing had been fulfilled.

~ Chapter 45 ~

"What do we do now?" Mungo asked eagerly. Owein had still not withdrawn from the lakeshore, though he now sat idly, every now and then doodling in its sandy mantle.

"What does your Book say?" Owein murmured flatly.

Mungo shook his head dramatically. "Nothin' – we still haven't reached Volume Eight, when Shailana and Tur are reunited. So we're still in the bit that's missin'." After failing to elicit acknowledgement, Mungo continued more peremptorily, "It's *your* Book, Y'r Highness – I gave it to *you*."

"'Highness'," Owein echoed sardonically, shaking his head. He looked up from the sandy shore out across the surface of the water, which still rippled softly.

"Shouldn't you go back to Wetherstag?" Mungo suggested, throwing his hands to the ground in exasperation.

"How can I return?" Owein replied morosely. "I am less a king now than when I left – no longer a king in waiting, merely a disgraced pretender. No, I will wait here to die – whether by hunger, age, or a Durdish sword, it matters not. I thank you for your services, my friend. I suggest you flee this bitter land and retire to Brambia before the rest of the world is annihilated. Perhaps Elyon will suffer a whim of mercy and spare that happy country."

"Beggin' your pardon, Y'r Highness, but I've already left you once, and I ain't doin' that again." Mungo marched deliberately to Owein's side and joined him on the soggy ground.

Owein smiled tenderly. "If I recall, it was I who left you."

The pair sat together speechlessly until Mungo punctured the silence. "Last time we was sittin' together by the wat'r, you had just washed up at Lanercost. Somehow I think we're supposed to be here." Having yet to release the psalter from his grasp, Mungo duly proffered it to Owein, who hesitantly accepted.

Instantly, their ears were perked by the unmistakable resonance of hoofsteps, which ricocheted around the encompassing mountainsides. The duo swivelled frenetically to locate the source of the disturbance: an armoured troop approaching from the opposite valley.

Mungo sprang to his feet. "Come on!" he urged, "we need to get away or else we'll get caught!"

"It's too late," Owein replied assertively, rousing from his depression. "More than likely they've already spotted us, and we'll never outrun them on foot. Our only chance is to play the innocent." Owein rummaged through his sack to produce two half-length casting poles which they had scavenged at Lanercost, handing one to Mungo. "We are just local fishermen. I could use a morsel anyway," he quipped, trying to calm his partner's nerves.

The pair waited nervously as the corps approached along the lake. "If they engage us in dialogue, it would probably be best if it is I who speak," Owein suggested. "Your accent might betray that we are foreigners." Mungo nodded vigorously in agreement.

Owein's veneer of nonchalance evaporated when he espied the unit's banner: a silver birch tree imposed on a deep-blue scrim. "The royal entourage," he murmured grimly. "It's Dunragit." Unnerved, Mungo began to resubmit his plea to flee but was immediately silenced. "If we run we'll be hounded and slain. Stay where you are – and act natural."

It was not long before Owein and Mungo found themselves encircled by a forest of spearheads, prompting Owein to climb to his feet and Mungo to jettison his fishing rod. The lead rider initiated the confrontation. "Bedwas Owein, son of my father's assassin!"

~ Chapter 46 ~

Urien climbed down to the place where he had delivered Trusmadoor, turning from there to the new shoreline, certain now that the bargain had been kept, that the Cornerstone would await him. It was then that he noticed a solitary starling, having withdrawn from the flock, capering daintily around a shallow pool and every so often pecking at its contents. He knelt down beside the puddle to find a solitary oyster, surrendered by the uncursed sea, basking in the morning sun. As he took the shelled prize into his hands, the winged messenger fluttered away across the sea to rejoin the diaspora. Gently, he pried open the earthen vessel to discover a heavenly treasure – a white pearl, a perfect sphere, shining with the same untainted, iridescent light he had beheld in the presence of the Shai. Urien had found the crown jewel of Shainor, the Mountain of Mist from which all waters flow; he had found the Cornerstone.

Urien sauntered along the coastline, pondering as he went. The final stage of his quest was to return the Cornerstone to Shailana; but how to reach that fabled place, if even it was a place, let alone one that could be reached? Had he known the answer to that question, he would not have spent precious time wandering the lengths and breadths of Tur in search of enchanted caves and mysterious artefacts. Yet he knew better than to doubt: the Way must be walked, and he had walked in it; and though he had stumbled, he had not been allowed to fall.

To placate his restlessness, he alighted on a smooth boulder and examined the oyster, which he had yet to discard. Separated from its aquatic life-source, the gentle creature had already begun a gradual process of mortification; it had fulfilled its purpose and would expire within a week. Its legacy, though, would be eternal, its payload priceless, its story told across the world.

~ Chapter 47 ~

"Whatever your business here, Usurper King, explain it quickly – or it shall be hastily ended."

Owein stared back at his enemy with furrowed brow and sealed mouth. Mungo's attention, meanwhile, oscillated frantically between the two kings, his own brow raised and his mouth ajar.

Dunragit dismounted his horse, drew his sword, and levelled it at Owein, peering down the fuller as if to take aim. After failing to elicit a response, he pivoted the weapon toward Mungo. "I will start with your minion here, if you'd prefer."

Owein did not fear the weapon, though he did envy it, so that his defiance was only inflamed. "My minion indeed," he sneered in the most derisive tone he could muster. "A Durdish ninny whom I pressed into servitude – and now a traitor by your own law. Should he not then face the humiliation of Carleol Square rather than be executed here, where none can witness his punishment?" Mungo glanced disbelievingly at Owein, who restrained himself from meeting his companion's eyes. He knew that Mungo would not understand the ploy.

"Perhaps," the king-at-arms agreed sinisterly, "after we pry your insidious mission from his simple mind. But you, Owein the Usurper, son of Urien the Conspirator, will die here, where Alba itself fell to ruin." With that pronouncement, Dunragit raised the weapon above his head, the bedevilment of vengeance contorting his face.

"Stop!" cried a deep, female voice as Maran Osla emerged from the encircling guardsmen, "I implore you, Sire, hear my counsel!"

Dunragit lowered his sword, but kept it in battle position. "It had better be forthright and forthcoming, Maran, for this criminal is ready to receive his sentence."

"Remember why we are here, Your Highness," Osla exhorted with calculated poise.

Lowering his guard, this time fully, Dunragit turned toward the water, watching as it weaved its intricate fabrics of fluid, flux, and flow. Under his breath, he recited to himself:

> "Where the ashes of the world are spread,
> And the world itself weeps o'er the dead –
> At Crummock will your Redeemer wait
> The very world to liberate."

As if snapping out of a trance, he turned abruptly back to his captive. "This fiend is anything but the Redeemer," he snarled, again pointing with his sword. "On the contrary, liberation would be accomplished by eliminating the tyrant."

"Tell us why you are here, Rhegedon," Osla urged Owein.

Owein remained impassive, as if to invite his own execution. Mungo's restraint, though, was finally depleted. "We are here to fulfil the Prophecy of Enoch," he declared in his thick, rustic pronounciation. "This is the King of Righteousness."

"Ha!" Dunragit spewed. "And I suppose you would claim to be the

Acolyte. You insult us."

Osla took another step forward. "With respect, Sire, we should keep these two alive. At the very least they will afford us valuable information – not to mention leverage."

Dunragit glared at Owein as he considered the appeal. "Very well," he eventually conceded, begrudgingly thrusting his sword back into its sheath, "this place of tears will be spared further bereavement for today." As he walked back to his horse, he scanned the surrounding peaks as if to deliver a parting shot. "This place has enough reason to weep."

~ Chapter 48 ~

"Would you insult me also, Maran?" Dunragit bristled as he bobbed in his saddle. He was leading the royal guard back to Mallerstang at walking pace, his two prisoners tethered to the rearmost rider. "I should treat such irreverence with severity, did I not hold your counsel in such high esteem."

Osla responded with balanced probity. "If you do esteem my counsel, Sire, then consider it now, I entreat you. Let us not forget the words of the Culdee Covenant."

Berlewen Hoel, riding on the opposite side of Dunragit, submitted the relevant scripture:

> "A Keeper will he be
> in Priestly company;
> A king without a crown,
> A sunrise going down;
> A stranger whom you know,
> A friendly sort of foe;
> A flower yet to bud,
> He shed and shares your blood."

"Bedwas Owein is no Keeper," Dunragit asserted unequivocally, barely keeping his temper in check. "Nor is that fool of his a Priest."

"Yet otherwise he conforms to the description," Osla countered, making sure not to negate Dunragit's statements. "His kingship lacks ordination, and he is affianced to your relative. Not to mention his

176

threadbare clothing – if he is a flower, he is certainly yet to bud."

"And the servant does speak in a strange way," Hoel added reflectively. "It does seem most uncanny that we would find Owein here, unguarded, on this day. Maran's explanation is difficult to accept, but pure coincidence is surely more preposterous still."

Dunragit weighed the evidence with a scale skewed by resentment. "Owein has shed enough of my people's blood – that much is for certain. Indeed, it was his armies that scorched the Wood of Shamayim, just as Gorsedd Cadell's armies scorched the Isle of Tiree in the last age. The Rhegedons are destroyers of the Land, not its Keepers. To suggest otherwise is both farcical and profane."

"Yet the Birch of Ibar endured when Albion burned the forest," Osla reminded him solicitously. "Its appearance was what led us here, was it not?"

"You need not remind me of the Oracle, Maran – I witnessed its fulfillment with my own eyes." As if he were once again peering across the surface of Crummock, Dunragit recited, again under his breath:

> "The Silver Birch will be refined by the fire of Heaven;
> It will withstand the flame that consumes the dross of the earth.
> The Tree of Ibar will appear like a spire from Heaven;
> In a scorched place, it will draw the nations across the earth.
> Then the One Land will be resurrected, its shrouds cast off,
> Until the Seven Winds are released, and all is blown away.
> Then all bonds will be loosed, yokes undone, oppressors

thrown off,

Until All is One, and Heaven and earth have passed away."

The riders fell silent as they continued to Mallerstang.

~ Chapter 49 ~

By the time Mallerstang came into sight, the hostages were barely able to stand on their aching, blistered feet. Mungo's distress was visible – and audible, too, until it was silenced by the back of a soldier's steel-plated hand. Owein, by contrast, refused to display his exhaustion.

Heedless of their plight, Dunragit was spurred by the appearance of their destination. "We must see my sister immediately," he stated tersely to his advisors, who were themselves beginning to flag. "The coming of Ibar's Tree heralds victory for Durdich, yet Albion has us on our knees. Breaca will know how to proceed."

Hoel sighed with sulky lassitude. He had whined nearly as much as Mungo. "What of the prisoners?"

"The bumpkin will be imprisoned in Bashan," Dunragit instructed disdainfully, "at least until I determine what to do with him. Throw him in with Beggerin – perhaps the two traitors will kill each other and save me the bother."

"And the Rhegedon?" Osla queried hesitantly, mindful that she had already tested the King's patience.

Dunragit turned halfway round in his saddle towards the captives, wrestling between wisdom and revenge. "You are right, Osla, we should first discharge our cargo. Our people are weary and discontented," he concluded upon resetting. "The capture of Owein the Usurper will bring them some needed revelry. Put him on the

Mast."

"Should we not first discuss his fate with Breaca?" reacted Osla, this time failing to contain her passion.

"You will find yourself in Bashan if you are not careful, Maran Osla!" Dunragit flashed back, startling his horse into a sudden lurch. After realigning his posture, he continued more calmly. "Given the recent spate of treachery, you would do well not to invite my suspicion. Your integrity over the years has persuaded me to overlook your Rhegish origins, but I have not forgotten them." Dunragit again peered back to his precious cargo, this time turning fully. "Besides, Bedwas Owein will not be going anywhere."

~ Chapter 50 ~

The Mast was the vestige of an ancient galleon, one of the few remaining traces of an age when the limits of Tur were not the limits of the world. Salvaged from the drained coastline of Lanercost, the colonial rulers had erected it in Mallerstang's Carleol Square as both a podium and a pillory. As a public display of humiliation, delinquents would be cooped up in the crow's nest, which the consuls would alternately use to issue notices and promulgate decrees. Like the balcony above the Round Table, Drochduil had retained the landmark as a reminder of Rheged's oppression, and like the balcony it was no longer used. Now, it would hold the oppressor himself.

Upon reaching the city's encircling walls, Dunragit immediately ordered the gatekeepers to deliver the Trumpet Call of Mallerstang. The Call could be raised by the King or his designated messenger at any of the city's seven gates: the Gate of Heaven and Earth; the Gate of Wisdom and Deception; the Gate of Peace and War; the Gate of Light and Dark; the Gate of Water and Drought; the Gate of Sea and Blood – and the Gate of Tree and Fire, where Dunragit's coterie had arrived. Once raised, the Call would be carried sunwise from one gate to another in turn until it reached the original gate, with all trumpets, including the original trumpet, sounding lower than the one before. A final call would then commence, again beginning with the original gate and proceeding in a circular fashion; but this time, each trumpet would hold its note until all seven trumpets were sounding in unison to produce a complete, symphonious octave. By the time the final call had ended, all the city's inhabitants were to have gathered in Carleol Square to await the King's address.

Dunragit accelerated toward the Square as the crescendo began. His troupe, constrained by the pace of their exhausted hostages, trailed behind.

~ Chapter 51 ~

Dunragit's coterie, minus Mungo and the soldiers assigned to him, arrived as the first round of trumpet calls was finishing. Along with the unit of guards which surrounded the Square, a multitude of malnourished, malcontented souls, mainly young and elderly, had assembled to face the rostrum from which royal decrees were customarily delivered.

"The King!" somebody shouted as the royal banner streamed through one of the Square's seven passageways, each of which originated at one the city's seven gates. "Here comes the King!"

After swivelling their heads to verify the announcement, the crowd fell to their knees in perfunctory submission and the square fell silent. Unexpectedly, Dunragit proceeded to the Mast, which lay on the opposite side of the Square to the rostrum. The war-weary, battle-scarred audience stood and hesitantly followed, shuffling and drifting in the glum expectation of ill tidings. The King halted beside a frayed rope ladder; it dangled from the monument like a noose, swaying in the wind like a ghost of antiquity.

When the final trumpet call commenced, Dunragit dismounted, gesturing to the rearguard for the captive to be brought forward. The mob watched in bewilderment as the King forced Owein up the pendulous ladder before ascending himself, grappling with the rickety rungs. Hoel followed without invitation or permission. Owein, meanwhile, was too spent by the recent journey to worry about the precariousness of the climb, depending as it did on rotten wood and brittle rope; but the timeworn artifact held them, despite its creaks and groans. The trumpet call had nearly peaked by the time they reached the crow's nest, as the last of the townspeople percolated into the Square.

When the crescendo terminated, the city was silent on pain of death. Dunragit moved to the edge of the platform while Hoel supervised Owein, who had yet to stand after exerting the last of his energy on the ascent. The Durdish King clasped the splintered banner which girded the balcony, envisioning the generations of Rhegish consuls who had stood there to subjugate the very people who now looked to his strength, on account of the very bloodline which now lay at his mercy. In the distance, he could discern the Beryl Sea, perceiving for the first time that its tides had subsided. "Alba", he whispered to himself, once again passing into a state of brooding absorption. "The One Land is being reborn."

Dunragit began to roam assuredly across the platform with his hands folded behind him, as if he were back in his throne room consulting his councillors. "People of Durdich," he exclaimed, his voice loud and orotund, like the deepest of the trumpet calls. "People of the One Land. I stand before you now, in this place, because it was ordained by the Keeper of Keepers that here, today, we should together witness the dawning of a new age, of a new world."

Dunragit let his words resound around the Square before continuing. "I know your pain. I know your grief, your despair, your weariness. I know that you have lost children, parents, siblings, spouses. I know that many of you have lost hope.

"Each day I remember my own father, Bassien Conlaoch. I remember his honour, his wisdom, his strength. I remember his mighty deeds, his visionary leadership, his love for Durdich. And I remember his betrayal at the hands of Urien the Conspirator.

"You have seen our Land defiled and disgraced. The massacre of Brackentrod, the devastation of Tiree, the countless depredations of Gorsedd Cadell and his would-be heirs. From this very Mast, the Empire has tyrannised our nation and profaned our religion.

"I bear these iniquities like a millstone around my neck. Not a moment passes in which I forget the weight of my duty – the duty passed to me from the Keepers of Alba, from Ibar Drochduil, from Bassien Conlaoch. They watch me from the Lost Land, where your fathers also wait for justice.

"Long have we suffered the injustices of Rheged. But no longer! For today is a day of reckoning. It is a glorious day, a joyous day, a scarlet day. It is the day which our forefathers foretold and for which we have hoped these long, painful years."

Having intensified into a bellicose war-cry, Dunragit's oration now became deliberate and enunciative, his voice lower in pitch and richer in texture. "I tell you, hear me now: I have seen the Silver Birch of Ibar, standing like a spire from Heaven in a scorched place." His eyes widened, as if he were beholding the omen there and then. "In the Wood of Shamayim it stood, enduring the fiery ruination of the armies

185

of Andras Albion. Yes, I tell you, with the Land as my witness, the Oracle has been fulfilled!"

Whereas the myths of Rheged had long since faded into obscurity, becoming the preserve of cranks and academics, those of Durdich were cherished by the common man – and had been since they were first conceived. The Oracle of Ayla, the Culdee Covenant, and other sacred creeds all emerged after the dissolution of the Kingdom as a syncretism of Rhegish legend and folk religion. Faith, however, had been eroded by generations of hope deferred, and the crowd responded to the announcement with guarded, equivocal stares.

Dunragit was unperturbed by the impassivity, for his proclamation issued from unwavering conviction. "Fate has imparted us surety for this promise," he pontificated, returning to his original grandiloquence. "A foretaste of our approaching victory."

Dunragit motioned to Hoel for Owein to be brought forward. "The man before you is none other than the perpetrator of our oppression, the culprit of our miseries." His ardour escalated into a strident roar as he prowled back and forth behind his prey, measuring it with contempt and revulsion. "This stinking, beggarly beast is the very demon who has haunted our waking and sleeping hours, who has made our lives a torment! The blood of Durdich is on his hands!"

The onlookers exchanged bemused expressions. "It can't be Albion?" somebody muttered incredulously. "Perhaps it's Beggerin," another suggested, "I heard they finally did him in."

Dunragit drew his sword theatrically from its sheath and aimed it menacingly at the hostage. With unrestrained zeal, he exclaimed, "I give you Bedwas Owein, the Usurper King of Rheged!"

The congregation erupted with compounded catharsis, the outcry mutating between euphoric cheers and vitriolic jeers. Raising his head and arms to the sky as if to bask in the glory of the moment, Dunragit bellowed over the rhapsody: "I tell you again, O nation of valiant men, O country of noble women – O Land of Lakes, O Land of Lands – the Oracle has been fulfilled! Today is the the day of our liberation! Here is the place of our deliverance!"

The jubilation reached fever pitch. Turning purposefully from the stage, Dunragit spoke into Hoel's ear before starting down the ladder. The Master duly bound the prisoner to the backbone of the Mast using a stray length of rope, one of countless that strewed the skeletal structure like cords of Spanish moss. Drunk with vengeance, the crowd proceeded to assail the prisoner with all manner of projectiles, raided from the market stalls which littered the Square.

As Dunragit looked down from his teetering descent, his peripheral vision, tinted with instinctive suspicion, detected a lone figure moving anomalously toward the edge of the Square. He watched with premeditated rancour as Maran Osla headed surreptitiously down a deserted alley. Dunragit knew that it led straight to the Gate of Wisdom – and to his sister, Ayla Breaca.

~ **Chapter 52** ~

The last time Owein was confined to a vessel of the sea, it was of his own accord. The three days that he had spent in that wooden coracle had bridged the gap between word and world; having denied his physical flesh, he had reincarnated himself in the eternal language of Dalriada, the language by which all things live, and move, and have their being. As one who had both lived to die and died to live, he had then entered the land of his enemy to surrender his newfound kingship, his very personhood, to the blessed depths of the lake called *Crummock*. The curse had been broken; the Ancient Way had broken through.

Now he found himself bound once more to an archaic ark, only this time he was shipwrecked inland in the land of his enemy. The Mast was littered with sticks and stones, comestibles and excrement, and even the odd shoe – anything that the townspeople could find to assail the captive. A few still loitered in the square below, waiting for further amusement or using the assembly as a chance for chitchat. Owein was unable to stand for agony and frailty; his blisters had suppurated and his stamina had dissipated. His muscles ached and his joints seized; it was if there was nothing between his withering bones and his wilting skin. What more was to be done, and what more was there to give? Had he not accomplished his mission? Why had the Kingdom not been restored?

The Kingdom. Owein extracted Feolan's acorn from his chest pocket and cradled it in his palm. *The Kingdom is now in your hand.* He passed his thumb over the cupule – a sort of dainty beret, with its overhanging rim and crowning nub. Yes, it was a crown, like the crown of Rheged that would never sit on Owein's head.

Then Owein realised: it was the Diadem.

~ Chapter 53 ~

"Are you also here to die?"

Mungo had assumed he was alone. The dungeon was completely dark except for a murky glow, which seemed to emanate from nowhere and served to reveal nothing. Startled, he turned to behold a mangled figure limping laboriously toward him.

"That's the only reason anyone is ever sent to Bashan," the faceless voice explained, "to be forgotten and, sooner or later, to die."

As the figure approached, a faint impression of his fungal features came into view. He seemed to belong to the punitive underworld, as if it were his native habitat, as if he had been bred in its eerie mildew and its desolate shadow. Mungo stared at the gruesome creature with jaw agape, in fascination though not in fear.

"Or have you already died?" the prisoner quipped, amused by Mungo's dumbfounded reaction. "Or perhaps, like me, that is what you are trying to deduce."

Mungo snapped back to attention. "No sir, I ain't dead," he asserted , shaking his head as if to assure himself. "I'm alive."

"Ah, good!" the hunchback declared wryly, "it is not good to die alone, after all."

He was now standing close enough that Mungo could distinguish his misshapen frame. "If you don't mind me askin', sir, why's your back so crooked?"

The cripple weighed the unexpected question before answering with remorseful pride. "I was felled in battle while protecting my king, Bassien Conlaoch. I was crushed under the weight of my own horse."

Mungo's interest was piqued. "And how did you end up here, seein' as how you were so brave?"

Beggerin grinned at the innocence of the questioner, but duly grimaced at the solemnity of the question. "My bravery was rewarded with land, wealth, and titles. I developed an appetite for the trappings of power – an insatiable appetite, a deceptive appetite. Now I am receiving my just reward." The penitent had evidently accepted his guilt and confronted his shame; yet, having already enjoyed ample time in which to dwell on his transgressions, he was inclined to change the subject. "And you – how did you become imprisoned so far from home? For I discern that you are a Brambian."

"I was also tryin' to help a king." Mungo sank to the ground in despondent frustration and began fiddling with the grimy stonework. "Didn't do any good, though."

"Your intention was good, and that is all too rare in these darkest of days." Beggerin's consolation was accompanied by a kind of fatalistic dejection. "Whether you succeeded matters not. We shall all of us perish, for Durdich is overrun."

Mungo looked up pertly from his idle enterprise. "But we'll all live again in the New World." As if struck by the disappointment of the prevailing situation, he again concerned himself with the intricacies of the dusty floor. "At least, that's what me Nana used to say."

Beggerin grinned again. "I see in you my former self, young Brambian. Here," he said with a raspy, affectionate voice, revealing a solitary key from under his cloak. "Flee this wretched place, and never look back. Perhaps you can escape the destruction to come."

Mungo grasped the key in disbelief. He had watched in helpless distress as the guard wielded that very instrument to incarcerate him in his present darkness. "How did you get this?"

"I've been a servant of the crown for longer than Dunragit's been alive," Beggerin preened, his smile stretching into a smirk. "I know my way around."

Mungo oscillated apprehensively between the gift and its giver, considering the bequest with plaintive appreciation. "Why don't you come, too?"

"I am a traitor," Beggerin replied stoically. "I will not absolve myself through further treachery. You, on the other hand, are innocent, unless I'm not Beggerin Achill." A pang of poignancy suddenly penetrated his defences. "But remember me in your New World, I pray, if you ever find it."

Mungo was stirred by the sequence of contrition and hope. "I won't need to remember you, Beggerin Achill," he promised tenderly, 'cause you'll be there too. We'll all be there."

Beggerin curled his reptilian lips into a crescent of acceptance – his final grin in the Old World, which, along with his old life, was passing away. "Go with Elah, young Brambian."

~ Chapter 54 ~

The last few days had been enough to drive even someone as level-headed as Maran Osla to insanity; and by the time she arrived at the sanatorium, she was inclined to admit herself into its custody. She was there to see Ayla Breaca, sister of the king who now threatened to undo the Oracle – and fiancée of the king who promised to fulfil it. It was Breaca's forerunner, Ayla Talwyn, who had first presaged the appearance of Ibar's Tree and the restoration of the One Land. At that time, the Priory of Ayla was regarded as a convent, its sisters revered as mystics, prophets, and savants, their counsel treasured as divine inspiration. But after generations of disappointment and embitterment, the Priory had been reduced to a prison, its inmates despised as lunatics – or worse, condemned as witches.

Despite her haste, Osla stole a moment to admire the magnificent but neglected building – the Sun Hall, so named for its distinctive layout of oblong vestibules emanating like rays from a circular nucleus. Sitting astride the Gate of Wisdom, it was a city within the city – a kind of omphalic microcosm, a sort of cartographic miniature which mapped the elemental features of mind and matter. It was the end of the circle, where echoes and reflections came first in the emergent surprise of new creation; it was the eye of the earth, the cradle of the world. It was a crown; it was a cornerstone.

In days gone by, a clerk would have attended to visitors, but Osla entered unescorted. Breaca was sitting expectantly in the middle chamber, where draped cenobites drifted by in slumberous contemplation.

"Breaca," Osla hailed, dispensing with pleasantries. "Dunragit is here. He has captured Bedwas Owein."

"Osla," Breaca reciprocated blithesomely, "my dear friend. Have some tea," she insisted, offering a steaming cup from the adjacent table. "It will calm your nerves."

Osla was inclined to decline the refreshment until she encountered its earthy aroma of catnip and chamomile, which slew her senses with transcendent peace. Almost involuntarily, she sat down across from Breaca and accepted the gift.

Breaca poured herself a cup of the narcotic nectar. "It is good to see you, my dear friend. Now," she intoned with warmhearted satisfaction, like a great aunt delighting in her favourite child, "tell me why you are here."

Osla proceeded to recount the discovery of Owein and Mungo, their uncanny conformance to the descriptions of the Covenant, and Dunragit's refusal to see beyond his own glory and revenge.

Breaca placed her empty cup on the table with serene meditation. Her mien of mastery belied her comparative youth, which was nevertheless apparent in her bright, incisive eyes. "You believe this Rhegedon to be the Redeemer – the one who will fulfil the Oracle."

Osla had not yet dared to formulate her discernment into a statement of truth; to hear it aloud was disconcerting. "Is he?" she asked after a few moments of hesitation.

One of the reasons that the House of Ayla had been forsaken lay in its offensive, sacrilegious merger of Rhegish and Durdish mythologies. Its soothsayings had originally been exploited for their jingoistic, insurrectionary appeal; and yet the sayers themselves had always insisted that all of Tur would share in the coming salvation. The One Land of Alba, the Old Kingdom of Rheged, the Ancient Way of Dalriada – all of these were revelations of the same unfolding mystery, recollections of the same undying memory. The Priory's vision of reconciliation was a thorn in the side of an increasingly militaristic regime, and was accordingly disdained, discredited, and discarded.

Breaca smiled wildly as she rebounded the question. "Did you know that there is a house in Wetherstag identical to this one? It was there that the old Rhegish bards penned the Lindisfarne Chronicles, amongst other sacred texts. Not even Gorsedd Cadell dared desecrate these sanctuaries." Osla could not help but marvel at the bastion of beatitude as Breaca extolled it, full of poverty and purity, of goodness and grief. "It is said that both buildings were built by the Shai, or even the Keepers. Or perhaps they were the same people. Perhaps," she tendered in a bewitching, provocative timbre, "they are us."

Osla struggled to contain her impatience. Though she respected Breaca more than anyone, along with her unorthodox wisdom, Osla was herself a woman of realism and practicality. "What of Owein?"

Breaca accepted the plea for frankness. "There is a prophecy which foretells of a day when Rheged and Dalriada will become one, when

196

their kings will once again follow in the Ancient Way." Breaca refilled both of their cups as she continued. "You know it well, my dear friend."

Maran Osla traced her ancestry to the bridge city of Glaramara, before it was a border – indeed, before there was such thing as a border save the bridgeless threshold of sea. With the disunion of the kingdoms, her family was likewise disunited – an injustice which, despite her noble status, she had carried in her blood, in her bones, in her very being. She was a woman of Durdich, but also of Rheged, and she would never be at peace as long as the Land was divided.

"The Prophecy of Enoch," Osla whispered tensely. It was Breaca who had taught her the Rhegish prophecies, which were outlawed in the realm of Durdich under pain of death. Osla already felt that pain – it was the pain of remembering the thousands who had already died and the thousands more who were now marching to their deaths.

Perceiving that Osla's passion was kindled, Breaca stoked the fire. "The Prophecy speaks of a Diadem," she prompted.

Uneasily but ardently, Osla recited the pertinent verse:

> "The Diadem interred in earth
> The Cornerstone raised up to Heaven;
> What is above and what is below
> Will be rebirthed as one expression
> Of perfect love, its perfect flow,
> And out of love the New World will grow.
> Look to the Doves and the blessed Rainbow."

Breaca was gratified by the testimony. "We, too, await the coming of the New World," she professed prayerfully, beholding the air around her as if that world could arrive from anywhere at any moment.

As if to provide a third witness, a wandering sister chanted as she passed:

> "The rough made smooth, the kingly common
> The world made new from top to bottom;
> So it shall be when Ibar's Tree
> Reveals the King, the only begotten."

Content that Osla was ready for the answer she sought, Breaca finally granted it. "Ibar's Tree is close at hand, for the Diadem is here." Again, she surveyed the atmosphere with beatific expectation. "Yes, the season is nigh, for time is catching up – and places are converging."

~ Chapter 55 ~

It was a common night in the city of Ravenshield, which lay between two of the numberless, nameless mountains of the Abaddon range. As the heat rose from the earth to the heavens, the water in the air would condense into fog or cloud, which would linger in the valley until the morning sun once again warmed the ground. In the winter months, when the nights were long and the sun was weak, the low cloud could last for days, casting the city into a disorienting stupor. Inhabitants would feel neither asleep nor awake as they drifted through the streets like ghosts.

The midnight watch was caught off-guard when the imposing figure of the High Commander of Rheged suddenly appeared, riding in full gallop along the King's Road. The veil of mist and murk had concealed his approach until he was within a stone's throw of the city's perimeter; he emerged as if from nowhere, as if the gates of hell had been opened, as if Armageddon was at hand. The archers tautened their bows, taking aim at the apparent aggressor.

"Hold!" exclaimed Hruden Raman, who was directing the watch. "He bears the peace-birds!"

Sure enough, the pennant fluttering from the rider's pole bore not the golden oak and scarlet scrim of Rheged, but the ivory Doves of Shekinah, following each other forever to the Highest Heaven.

Unable to sleep, Dahaka Ram had been strolling ambivalently along the interim front, gazing westward into the night as he anticipated the morrow's battle. He arrived swiftly to address the disturbance. "The High Commander," he identified curiously. "He rides alone?"

"Yes," Hruden replied jitterously, fighting to maintain his composure.

After letting the situation reveal itself to him, Dahaka withdrew towards the barracks. "Bring him to my quarters," he ordered.

***

When the colossus of a man bowed to his host, it seemed as if the room bowed with him. "I am Maran Atha, High Commander of Rheged."

Dahaka stood with his hands folded behind his back and his brow folded over his eyes, as if he had somehow expected the encounter but was nevertheless perplexed by it. "Yes, I know who you are. What I do not know is why you are here."

"I come to plead for peace," the High Commander responded, the deep vibrations of his voice reflecting the gravity of his statement.

Dahaka remained circumspect. "You accepted great danger to come here, Maran Atha. My archers nearly turned you into a pin cushion." Dahaka turned to inspect one of the marble busts which graced the room. He wondered whether one of his own ancestors had ever known the man it immortalised. "What of Aelhairn Urien? Why has he not come?"

The High Commander averted his steely eyes – first to the ground, as if mourning a tragic death, but then to the sky, as if reminded of a

200

distant hope. "King Urien is not here, for he has taken the road of pilgrimage – as has his son, Bedwas Owein. I come on their behalf."

Dahaka mulled over the revelation as he perused the gallery. The High Commander, he knew, was excluded from the line of surrogates by virtue of his Durdish origins. "Who keeps the city? For I hear that Malvern Brennus has been killed."

"Cullen Latrell is the next steward," Atha replied grievously, "but he has retreated to the West with as much wealth as he could carry. After him is Liadan Keir – but he bides in Glaramara."

Dahaka sensed an affinity with a man who was reproached for the blood in his veins, who was an alien in his own land, and yet who acted with honour, devotion, and magnanimity. "And you, Maran Atha – why have you not also retreated? We will take the city by noon."

The High Commander sighed in his spirit, as if he clung to an impossible promise. "King Urien believed that peace on Tur was yet possible – that goodwill could once again reign among men."

This time it was Dahaka who averted his eyes. He longed for peace more than life itself; indeed, he would give his life for it. Yet he served the people of Qahal; and he would not give any more of their lives in the name of peace, or any other promise made by those who had wed themselves to war. Dare he trust that this migrant king Urien was the Peaceful One, that his absent son was the first of the New Men? Tentatively, as if testing the water with the tip of his toe, Dahaka began to ask himself the question, resisting the instinct to recoil into fear and anger.

"And you, man of the March – do you believe it?"

The High Commander had been asking himself that question since Aelhairn Urien first left on his quest – indeed, since his own family was first split apart by a war which seemed as unstoppable as the waters of the Mara. "Yes."

~ Chapter 56 ~

When Mungo escaped the dungeon, his immediate concern was to locate Owein. That much, at least, had been straightforward: Bashan was situated next to the Gate of Peace and War, the nadir of one of the city's seven prime meridians which culminated in the zenith of Carleol Square. Mungo had followed the trajectory almost involuntarily, like a minor star gravitating in the orbit of a galactic giant. The Mast, moreover, was the cynosure of the constellation. Comers, goers, and idlers all marvelled at its wretched glory, praying that it spelled the healing of their wounds and the restoration of their Land, that the death of the counterfeit king would mark the beginning of a new life for their sons and their daughters.

The instant he beheld the scene, Mungo knew that these prayers would be answered. The heavenly spire, lifted up to reveal the king – this was the sign etched into the sacred writ which Owein himself carried in his pocket. The evidence was indisputable: they had passed through the scriptural intermission; Volume Eight of the Chronicles had finally arrived.

Instinctively and lovingly, Mungo yearned free his friend, to spare him his trial by fire. Plans of returning to the Square at night, of disguising himself as a palace guard, of creating various sorts of diversion, flashed through his mind. A childhood of mischief and tomfoolery perpetrated with his clownish accomplice Balder Appletree had at least trained him in the art of rustling, even if the rage of Farmer

Musgrave was somewhat more amusing than that of Bassien Dunragit. Yet he knew, in his self of selves, that the Chronicles had ordained for him a different path. If he really wanted to see the New World, he would have to forsake the man who had become to him a father.

***

"Why has Dahaka not advanced to Wetherstag?" Dunragit fumed as he patrolled his throne room, agonising over the perplexity. "It's been weeks since he took Ravenshield, and the Rhegs are all but spent." With a spiteful grin, he added, "Not to mention leaderless."

"It's those damnable Aramites," Hoel fired back, his prejudice excited. "I tell you again, Sire, the vermin are colluding with Brennus, or Latrell, or whichever Rhegish lowlife has survived their pitiful coup."

Dunragit hiked an eyebrow as if he had been presented with a mildly interesting trinket. "It has been reported that the High Commander has been directing operations – though," he droned dramatically, turning to flay Osla with his sharpened gaze, "his mongrel blood disqualifies him from acting as Surrogate."

Recalling Dunragit's arraignment of Beggerin, Osla resolved to keep her wits about her. Those wits, honed by a lifetime of practice, prompted her to address the issue head-on, to avoid any semblance of falsehood. "I have not seen Atha since I was ten years old, Sire, nor have I had any communication with him." She was reluctant to submit her next argument, perceiving its double-edged nature, but nonetheless assured herself that forthrightness was her strongest defence. "In any

204

case, the High Commander is a well-known dove – all the more so given his Durdish parentage. Any terms he may have reached with Dahaka are unlikely to involve a joint offensive against his motherland."

Dunragit reciprocated Osla's gesture of frankness. "What did Breaca say, Osla?" Mournfully, almost remorsefully, he added, "I know you visited her."

Fighting the impulse to feign ignorance, Osla quickly assembled a truthful yet innocuous account. "She told me that the Day of Redemption is near – that Owein's capture augurs the fulfillment of the Oracle."

Dunragit inhaled sharply, as if to dam a torrent of passion. He took a moment to savour the vision in his mind before returning to his original concern. "Mallerstang is safe, for Albion will not breach the southern belt. Even so, we are hard pressed on every side, for we hold neither Cromlech nor the Glen." He was now pacing again – this time more carefully, for he knew that history was watching him. "We must regain a foothold in Abaddon if we are to stake a claim in this wasting world, if we are to have a seat at the table of annihilation. It is there, in the mountains of destruction, that Alba will be born; for it is there that the enemies of Durdich will fall."

Osla and Hoel both waited in silent suspense, knowing that the Keeper King was spellbound beyond persuasion. Finally, he pronounced his judgement. "Prepare the army – we leave for Cromlech on the morn of the morrow."

"Yes, Sire," Hoel acknowledged with a spry bow.

The councillors were exiting the room to discharge the order when Dunragit halted them, once again sporting a hateful smirk. "Osla," he crooned artfully. "You shall lead the advance guard."

With a stiff nod, Osla assented. "Yes, Sire."

~ Chapter 57 ~

If pinching sheep from cantankerous farmers was one of Mungo's pastimes, escaping tight spots was undoubtedly one of his vocations – one which, much to his hilarity, poor Balder did not share. As per his craft, he had meticulously surveyed the lie of the land, scouting for blind spots and weak points. Alas, unlike Musgrave's farm or the Appletrees' orchard, the perimeter of Mallerstang was sealed in all places and guarded at all times. Even his uncanny knack for stealth and evasion could not avail him here.

Mungo had begun to wish that he was still in Bashan – at least in that prison he had received food, shelter, and, in Beggerin Achill, even a sort of company. In fact, he might well find himself there again, for he had reached the Gate of Wisdom and Deception. Though designed to repel external threats, the Gate was, like the other six, impassable even from the inside save by the will of the gatekeeper. Even if he could slip through one of the posterns or crawl under one of the culverts, Mungo would face acres of exposed ground before he was out of the watchmen's range. He would fare better at night, which would however present its own set of hazards, including bandits, beasts, and disorientation. Though he was not afraid of death, he was determined to reach Wetherstag alive, for the future of Tur depended on it.

"Mungo Caldbeck." The voice seemed to emanate from everywhere, resounding without tone or pitch; intangible yet ubiquitous, it was the harmony of Heaven that sustains the melody of earth. Mungo turned to behold a youthful Abbess, draped in a monochrome scapular and framed by an oversized coif. "I am glad you are here," she added, warmly yet assertively.

Mungo was certain he had never met the fantastic stranger; yet her demeanour was familiar, her bearing magnetic. "Ma'am," he replied queriously.

"I am Breaca," the prioress purred, "but my children call me Mother." Mungo felt her presence draw closer to him, though she remained still; indeed, it was her stillness that was palpable, for she seemed to be stiller than the rest of the world, as if she were present in all of it.

Breaca smiled affectionately at his confusion. "You seek a Way to Rheged," she said assuringly, "and to Dalriada." Mungo was immediately intrigued by the mention of his mission, though he was duly sobered by the memory of his master. It was Owein who had begun their communal journey, sacrificing first the comfort and security of his palace, then the glory and honour of his kingship, now the dignity and essence of his very humanity. Yet he would not witness its end, for he was its end; he was the fulfillment of the very prophecy that had impelled him to fulfill it.

"We will see him again in the New World," Breaca assured him, recognising Mungo's grief and partaking in it like a sacrament. "And we will see each other."

Mungo wept. He knew in his innermost being that it was the truth, but the cup of emptying would still have to be drunk; the blasphemy of dehumanisation would still have to be endured. Surrendering to the embraceful presence, he laid his head on her shoulder, resting on her living hope, receiving her comfort even as he mourned.

Breaca abided by the season, and abided in it; but once it had passed, she did not tarry. "Elah hears your tears, Mungo Caldbeck – and He will answer your cries." Gently yet decisively, she held his shoulders and stooped to meet his downward gaze. "But now you must go – for today is indeed the day of our liberation.

"You have circled the lake; now you must circle the city. You must leave behind your king, just as he left behind his kingship.

"The Gate of Heaven and Earth is opening. Go there, and consummate the wedlock."

Mungo pleaded with her through anointed eyes. Leaving her presence was nearly as difficult as leaving Owein.

"Go with Elah, my son," Breaca commissioned with a heartening warmth, "and do not fear; for the battle is already won."

***

When Mungo passed the Gate of Peace and War, with the Prison of Bashan at its base, he knew that the world had changed. Like the Trumpet Call of Mallerstang, his circumnavigation of the city had completed an octave; the Gate was now suspended in a higher tone of reality, in which the oppressiveness of Bashan no longer held sway. Its unwieldy portcullis was as indomitable as ever; yet even it was subject to the laws of the universe.

Mungo's attention, however, was captured by a surge of activity at his next milestone, the Gate of Heaven and Earth. A drumfire of hooves blended with a jangle of voices to evince unmistakably that the Army of the Land, the force charged with the final defence of king and country, had been marshalled. As Mungo scuttled toward the cavalcade, he discerned Maran Osla at the head of the formation, her commanding posture accentuated by her stately battledress. Authoritatively, she drew her sword and lifted it ahead of her, signalling for the Gate to be opened.

Mungo realised immediately that this was his chance to escape the city; but how could he join the formation without raising suspicion? His mind naturally flashed to Crummock, the corresponding circuit of which had led to their arrest. He recalled Osla's interventions when Dunragit was minded to slay them; though dispassionate, she had seemed intentionally charitable, as if she were concealing a treasonous sympathy. He concluded that he had no choice but to trust her.

To the protest of his nerves and veins, he scurried as far towards the gate as he could without attracting notice, before marching as naturally as possible to its near side. There he waited, fighting to dissemble his terror and praying that his imposture would be believed. When Osla's horse approached, he stepped in front and took hold of one of the reins, looking up at the rider to elicit her recognition.

At first she was bemused; but Mungo's shock of ginger hair, his spattering of freckles, and his childlike pair of eager eyes were difficult to forget. She blinked several times in a staccato rhythm as she registered the event and determined her response. Without breaking pace, she continued through the gate with Mungo escorting as a stablehand, masquerading as a servant of the king.

~ Chapter 58 ~

Urien had expected company. Aram lay at the mercy of the Onyx Sea, helpless against its vagaries and dependent on its vicissitudes. The premature subsidence of the ocean thus threatened the precarious subsistence of the people, who would, sooner or later, arrive to inspect the unseasonable shift.

When he spotted the first of the fisherman approaching from the South, Urien had stowed himself in the den which, colonised by barnacles and worn by waves, looked most likely to be disused. After vainly surveying the aberrant coastline, the fishermen had encamped in a nearby cluster. He envied their fire, their fare, and, most of all, their friendship; but he savoured the sound of human voices, rolling as they did with the soulful undulations of the ever-breaking sea.

The morning was punctuated by the arrival of a courier, evidently bearing urgent news. Urien could distinguish only three words from the frenzied conversation which ensued: "Dunragit", "Mallerstang", and "Owein". Rattled by the message, the fishermen hastily gathered their chattels and hightailed inland, gliding deftly over the lava fields. When they were far enough away, Urien moved over to their warren, devouring their abandoned breakfast before following their path towards the Mountains of Abaddon.

***

When the first city came into sight, Urien was struck by the juxtaposition of wilderness and metropolis. He assumed the conurbation to be Sychar, the high watermark of the Onyx Sea, marking the border of the great flood which covered the country each year at the time of Hanavi, reducing Aram to a mere strip of land between hell and high water. The mention of his son's name by the Aramite fishermen had compelled Urien to follow them here, yet his journey lacked purpose of plan. Knowing that he could not enter the city, he stopped in his tracks and removed the pearl from his satchel, where he had carefully swaddled it like an infant in a crib. He caressed its cornerless symmetry, its universal unity. Since discovering the treasure, he had come to realise that it had never been removed from the Heart of Shainor, for it could never be moved. No, it was the world which had moved. Rheged had rebuilt itself on a different foundation – not of dream, but of delusion, not of hope, but of obsession.

It was then that the air started to move; though, in truth, it felt as if it was the earth which was moving, as if the lava fields were melting beneath his feet. Urien perceived immediately that it was the Yom of Pesach, the Cry of Elai, distinguished by its saltiness, its sharpness, its bitterness. It was the same wind that his mind had conjured in the Desert of Shur to justify his transgression to the sheol; but this time it was no illusion. It was a wind encountered only by those who encounter death – those who are threshed in the final harvest to pass through the final threshold. That finality now thrashed against Urien's back like a scourge, penetrating his garments as if they were mere figments of his imagination.

Urien now understood his task. He must take the Cornerstone to

Wetherstag, for Owein was fulfilling the Prophecy of Enoch, the Culdee Covenant, and the Oracle of Ayla; he was bringing forth the New World. Urien recalled one of the verses engraved in the walls of Gwydir's cave:

> "Stand at the Oak, the tree of the Shai
> And you will be gone in the blink of an eye
> To the land past the sea,
> To the holy city,
> And the Mountain of Mist, the crown in the sky."

As Urien observed the monstrosity of Abaddon which lay before him, he knew that he could not return the way he had come. His only hope of reaching Wetherstag in time was the Valley of Golgotha.

~ Chapter 59 ~

Osla was used to hiding her emotions. Every day, though it felt like goring her finger into a half-healed wound, she would perform her duties with impeccable fidelity. Having an accomplice had briefly made the pretence more bearable, for it had affirmed her true allegiance, her true identity, reminding her that she was not in fact the mask she wore. The conspirators had bonded by circumstance, which had, withal, committed them to silence. She knew not the red-headed Priest's objective, or even who he was; but, judging by the frequency with which he glanced back towards the city, she could tell that his destination lay in the opposite direction.

At the first rest, she engaged her second-in-command. "I must send a message back to Mallerstang," she stated imperatively, raising her voice to ensure that it was overheard by the troops.

The lieutenant nodded mechanically, exhibiting a trace of surprise. "I will send a courier."

"No," Osla rejoined firmly, presenting him with a sealed parchment. "We need all the fighting men we have. Send the stablehand. And send him on foot – we need all the horses, too, and we are less than a day's trek from the city."

The lieutenant nodded again, this time more affirmatively. "You heard the Vicereine," he yapped at Mungo, thrusting the document towards him. "Best be on your way – the wolves come out at night, you know."

Mungo received the missive unsurely, unable to restrain himself from consulting Osla for answers. She, the more seasoned actor, furtively flicked her eyes as if to bid him leave, before turning away to other business. With his hands still cradling the scroll, Mungo duly obeyed the unspoken instruction, setting off southwards back towards Mallerstang.

***

It had not taken Mungo long to realise the purpose of the letter – namely to let him leave the camp. He would not have returned to Mallerstang anyway, for his sole preoccupation was now to reach Glenamara, where he planned to cross into Rheged. To do so, he would head westward to reach the Mara, which he would follow until it met the Emerald Sea.

The night was closing in when he happened upon a crossroad. In his haste, and in the dusk, he had not seen the pair of patrolmen guarding the way until he was within spitting distance – and, by then, he had already been seen. His initial instinct was to flee, but he thought better of it; after a day's journey, his chances of outrunning the sentinels were next to none.

"Oi, you there," one of them flashed, holding up a dim lantern and palming the hilt of his sword. "Not another step, or you'll be dinner for the wolves."

As Mungo complied with the order, the second soldier promptly demanded, "Speak your purpose here."

Mungo fumbled for an answer, rummaging through a jumble of thoughts. He was still holding Osla's letter. "I'm deliverin' a message on behalf of Vicereine Osla," he sputtered spontaneously, proffering the item for inspection. "I need to get to Glenamara."

The first soldier grabbed the parchment and held it up to his lamp. "It bears the seal of the Army of the Land," he observed approvingly, passing it to his colleague before directing the lantern at Mungo. "Dangerous to be out here alone. There's wolves in these parts, you know."

"Some in sheep's clothing," the second soldier sneered. "Rhegish spies everywhere nowadays. Caught three of them the other week, we did. Crossed the river on rafts, they did. Slashed their throats, we did."

Mungo swallowed squeamishly.

"He isn't even armed," the first soldier observed dismissively. "And besides, he's too simple to be a spy."

"True enough," the second jeered. "Can't even talk properly."

The first soldier lowered the lantern and stepped aside. "On you go," he conceded waspishly, as if addressing a naughty child, "and watch out for the wolves."

The second soldier snickered, thumping the parchment into Mungo's thumping chest and ruffling up his ruffled hair. "They have a taste for little red riding hoods."

***

If Osla had been his shepherd, she had delegated the function to an invigorating wind, which steered Mungo downriver as if the air and the water were manifestations of the same creative impulse. As life-giving as they were, they were leaving the world, for the First Moon of Winter had risen. The breath and pulse of the land were slowing, leaving its limbs cold and pale, its joints brittle and rigid, its skin coarse and slack. Yet there was a silent dignity of decay, of age embraced gracefully in the knowledge that the end is the beginning; that today will die, but tomorrow will live forever; that the empty darkness is the pupil through which all light is seen.

Mungo surmised the wind to be the Yom of Teruah, Elah's trumpet blast of arrival, of coronation, of victory. He was no king, but Mungo felt as if he was following in the way of his father, making the same pilgrimage, yearning for the same mystery. Indeed, the Prophecy of Enoch was nearly fulfilled; and, according to the Chronicles, he would have to reach Wetherstag, the pupil of the Old Kingdom, before the Tree of Ibar was revealed. Yet his journey was new; it belonged not to the things of old, but only to the ancient. It was the same rite through which his fathers had passed; yet the circle had become a spiral, just as all things under the sun are made new every morning.

Mungo ran through the night. Though he was wearied to the point of giddiness, reposing in the frigid darkness as an invitation for the fabled wolves was hardly more appealing. He understood that Osla had denied him a horse to avert suspicion; but now, as he forced his battered feet to strike the frozen ground again and again and again, he wished that she had not been so cautious.

When day broke, he was met by a stream of travellers – soldiers and civilians, men and women, old and young, migrating northward with the sum of their possessions loaded on carts and bundled in packs. Their expressions were exultant if exhausted, like a mother after giving birth. Mungo began to weave his way through the oncoming exodus, but the multitude seemed endless. Bemused, he accosted a passing widow.

"Beggin' your pardon, miss," he signalled courteously, "but where are all these folk headed?"

The matriarch looked up from beneath her bonnet. "To Mallerstang," she replied incredulously. "Why, haven't you heard? The Tree of Ibar's been found, and Bedwas Owein's been captured. The war's over, laddie."

***

Mungo had continued to encounter bands of expatriates, all exhibiting the same triumphal relief, all heading to witness the vindication of their age-old hardship. After nearly a week of tracking the Mara, however, he alighted upon a different sort of migrant, motivated not by the attraction of their destination but by the repulsion of their origin. Scores of refugees, terrorised and terrified, fled past him with nothing but the clothes on their backs and the trauma on their minds. Again, Mungo approached someone from the crowd, this time a father leading his wife and children.

"Beggin' your pardon, sir," he hailed politely, "where are all these folk comin' from?"

The mortified man did not even look at Mungo. "Albion," he croaked dejectedly, as if it was his last word before yielding to some inevitable, unthinkable fate.

Mungo's heart stopped. *Ibar's Tree is nearly here*, he admonished himself, recalling the fateful words of Enoch's Prophecy. He would have to hurry – and so would Urien.

***

Andras Albion's trail of destruction became increasingly evident as Mungo approached Glenamara. Crops, towns, and bodies all lay in smouldering spoils, through which the odd survivor trudged and combed as if unable to accept the magnitude of loss. The city itself, though scarred and bruised, was relatively unscathed, for Albion had considered it his child – to be toughened and chastened, but also cherished and protected. Nonetheless, Mungo had no misgivings about entering the city, for he had been there before.

"I'm a cousin of Liadan Keir," Mungo shouted pre-emptively as the sentries peered down from the walls. "I'm here to see him."

The watchmen exchanged apathetic shrugs and irritated sneers before one of them snapped his head to indicate an order. The recipient duly stood to attention before returning with the general.

"Ah, Mungo!" Liadan hailed from the parapet. His voice was falsetto, pinched, croupy, as if a lifetime of yelling had abraded his larynx. "Graben," he addressed to one of the guards, "open the gates, will you? This canny lad's me cousin!"

Liadan had descended to the gate by the time it opened. Like Mungo, he sported a thicket of ginger hair, but his stemmed from his face rather than his head. He was in fact completely bald, with a large port-wine birthmark bleeding down from his scalp across one of his two maniacal eyes.

"I'll be a son of a Priest," the wildman howled, biffing Mungo vigorously on the shoulder. "You're a strapping lad, aren't ya'?" Wrapping his burly arm around the stripling's neck, Liadan turned to his lieutenant. "I'll take a glass or two of what 'e's been drinkin', ya know what I mean?" As if he were already drunk, Liadan guffawed at his own joke; the soldiers responded with nervy imitation, as if they were expecting the werewolf to transmogrify.

Mercifully, Liadan released his victim. "Speakin' of which, you must have the Desert of Shur in that gob of yours. Let's get some ale in ya, lad," he insisted, slapping the prodigal nephew on his willowy back, "there's naught bett'r to do in this sheol of a town, anyhow."

Mungo stopped in his tracks, fondling the scroll in his pocket. "Actually, Finnian, I need to be goin'."

"'Finnian!'," he chortled resonantly. "Don't hear that name much anymore." The bystanding troops braced for one of their general's long-winded yarns about his boyhood in Brambia, before he was conscripted and forced to change his name. They sighed with relief when he overlooked the opportunity. "Not since you were here last, now that I think about it. How long ago was that, anyhow?"

Mungo opened his mouth to give an answer; but, to his own befuddlement, realised he did not have one. He had visited Finnian when Owein diverted to Kidron – that much he knew. But the entire spell between his master's departure and return seemed to be erased – not from his own memory, which was still intact, but rather from that of the universe.

"Ah well," Liadan declared casually, perceiving Mungo's distress. "At least call me Finn, for Elah's sake. Finnian's me father, ya know what I mean? Elah bless him," he reverently implored, putting his hand on his heart and glancing to the sky. "Anyhow, what brings you to the Glen this time? And for Elah's sake, why are you in such a rush?"

"I need to get to Wetherstag," Mungo sputtered restlessly, reminded of his urgent task. "It's the Prophecy of Melchizedek – Bedwas Owein – the Tree of Ibar – the –"

"Still chasin' stars and wives' tales, are ya'?" Liadan interrupted facetiously, striking Mungo's aching shoulder as he turned to his audience, who were evidently disquieted by Mungo's utterances. "Always causin' trouble, this lad. I reckon it's the 'barrow in 'im. His uncle Friggith's a sly devil, 'e is. Could sell sand in a desert, ya' know what I mean? And a canny cardshark, too. It was more'n a few times 'e took the clothes off me back. Aye, lost me finest mare to that rascal, I did. That's me cousin, mind; a Wakebarrow, 'e is. Always gettin' the bett'r of us Buckbarrows." The guards were grimacing now, realising that they were set to endure one of Liadan's mind-numbing anecdotes.

Graciously, they were saved by Mungo's intervention. "Speakin' of Morag, do you still have 'er?"

"Ah yes, of course, son," Liadan confirmed. "Been lookin' aft'r 'er meself, I have. It was me that bred 'er, ya know. Come, I'll take you to 'er meself." Liadan again headlocked his guest and began steering him through the open gate. "I tell ya', she's a Priest of a horse, that Morag. Still strong after all these years. Give me whatev'r she's been drinkin', ya' know what I mean?"

~ Chapter 60 ~

The Durdish territory once named after Rhainn Rhegedia, the Old Father of the Middle Land, was now a dismal no man's land. The soil was among the most fertile in Tur, enriched as it was by the volcanic mass of Abaddon. Yet it was those very mountains – the symbolisation of hostility in their diabolical contours, the prognostication of ruin in their minatory pinnacles – which deterred all but the bravest and most desperate of souls from abiding in their shadow. Now, their shuddersome profile loomed over the Army of the One Land, whose faltering advance was stifled by the irrepressible instinct that it was marching to its doom.

Osla knew what lay before them. The southern approach to Cromlech was less suicidal than the northern, which rose almost vertically from the abysmal canyon of Golgotha; yet the city was still a fortress, designed to repel the most forceful of invasions. The fear she felt was at once foreign and familiar: foreign, for to survive as Vicereine she had been compelled to estrange her inner child; and familiar, for that child waited incessantly at the door of her soul, crying for adoption, for acceptance, for security.

"A rider!" Osla's lieutenant was shouldering his way through the ranks to reach her. "A rider from Mallerstang!"

Osla pivoted her horse to look southward. Sure enough, a lone courier was galloping towards them, bearing the standard of Durdich. Osla motioned for the lieutenant to intercept him.

As soon as he arrived, the messenger disgorged his words in projectile spurts. "Albion has broken through the southern belt. He is less than a day from the capital. You must return at once to defend the city."

Osla glanced gravely in the direction of their origin. Under constant scrutiny as female councillor, and an ancestrally Rhegish one at that, she was in the habit of filtering, tempering, and otherwise editing her thoughts before expressing them in words. She was thus aware, to her own curiosity, that her reflexive concern was not for the king to whom she had sworn fealty, but rather for the king to whom she had, in so doing, sworn enmity. It was precisely such thoughts which she had spent a lifetime suppressing, worrying at all times that some seditious word would slip through her net. Now, she wondered whether she had been placed in her position for such a time as this.

"Order the retreat," she commanded the lieutenant decisively. "Full gallop."

As the lieutenant sounded a caterwauling horn to convey the order, Osla turned to the messenger. "How did Albion break through? More than half our forces are stationed in the south."

"Many of the towns were as good as abandoned by the time he arrived," the messenger replied incredulously, his adrenaline beginning to subside. "Everyone with the means had already left for Mallerstang — even the fighting men. They came to see Bedwas Owein."

***

After crossing the river, Mungo followed the Mara back towards the land with Morag to carry him, even as Owein had followed the Mull back towards the sea with Morag behind him. In the tedium of the journey, he itched to open Osla's letter, which he nestled in his inside pocket as a mother hen guards her brood. He knew that Osla had given it to him as a subterfuge, but somehow he knew that it bore a message of truth. If it was real, it should be treated as such: the Seal of the One Land was to be broken only by an Albar, a Keeper King.

Mungo had never been to Wetherstag; but as he caught sight of the city's whitewashed walls, he felt the same conflicted familiarity that one often feels when returning home after a long absence, after one has changed but the place has stayed the same. This was the city of the Old Fathers, yet it was blind; it had plucked out its own eyes by expelling its seers. This was the city of the Old Fathers, yet it was drunk; it had revelled in its riches only to be denuded and disgraced. This was the city of the Old Fathers, yet it was dead; it had hidden in the dark so long it fell asleep, a sleep too deep for rest or dream. Rheged needed the message that Mungo brought – but who in the city could open it?

And how would Mungo enter the city? He had entered Glenamara by pleading kinship, but this time he had no such cards to play. His relationship with the King would scarcely be believed; and, in any case, Owein had as many enemies as friends, even in the capital – especially in the capital. Mungo hoped, at least, not to be sniped by an archer; and he hoped, at best, to be put in prison. Perhaps he could once again escape, or feign madness, or swear allegiance, or reach the Garden of

Shemesh some other way.

Mungo felt his bowels quiver as a sentinel appeared on the parapet, immediately issuing the inevitable question. "Who goes there?"

Mungo groped the letter in his pocket, running his thumb over the waxy seal. He had no other ideas. "I've been sent by Vicereine Maran Osla," he proffered meekly.

The watchman glowered at him glassy-eyed, consulting an arbitrary space in the distance before withdrawing. The figure that returned was dark and robust, yet stricken and sallow – the High Commander.

Cautiously, he inquired in his staid, plummy voice, "You are acquainted with Maran Osla?"

***

The knowledge that they were heading for battle with Andras Albion was assuaged only by the knowledge that they were avoiding battle in the Mountains of Abaddon. Yet even this consolation was denied the Land's Army when a mounted force of Qa was spotted pursuing them from the fortress of Cromlech. The Qa carried no flag, for they had no country; yet for the same reason, they were more immediately distinguishable than the men of Tur. Their dress, their speech, their skin, their frame – all were remnants of another world.

"Curse the seas," the lieutenant profaned acridly, "the wolves have smelt blood. We're lambs to the slaughter out on these fields."

Osla rapidly assessed the situation. "We are closer to the city than they are to us," she noted forthrightly.

"Aye," the lieutenant remonstrated, "but their legs are fresh. They will surely catch us if we flee. Better to make a stand and meet them head-on than to invite their blades into our backs."

Osla weighed the argument. "We are closer to safety than you think. The Qa will not come within a mile of the city; for if they do, the Home Guard will send a force to repel them."

"We *are* the Home Guard," the lieutenant interjected, increasingly overwrought.

"Aye, but they aren't to know that." Osla's roguish response, which she accompanied with a sly smirk, was intended to allay the lieutenant's dread by disguising her own. She promptly concluded the exchange before the effect subsided. "Resound the retreat. Full gallop."

***

Mungo had not expected a man like the High Commander, prim and severe, to let him into the city, let alone the palace grounds. Still less did he expect such a man to break down in tears; but as the man of the Mara had wailed in disconsolate relief, Mungo could tell that he was a man of grief, acquainted with sorrows. The news that his sister had survived Dunragit's purge and yet was sentenced to suicide had disarmed him; it had demolished the barrier of temperament which, like his sister Osla, he had erected to withstand a constant barrage of envy, suspicion, and betrayal.

The High Commander's lament was prescient, for all barriers were about to be broken down.

***

The terrible rumble of their hunters' horses' hooves had mingled with that of their own to produce a continuous, ever-intensifying drone, a sort of prophetic requiem which welcomed them to the world beneath the ground. Every now and then, one of the soldiers would dare to look behind them, only to be transformed into a pillar of salt, pale and petrified. Yet it was the pillar before them which stopped them in their tracks, causing their hearts to beat as quickly as the hooves: a vast billow of smoke, dark as the skin of their pursuers, originating from their destination. It was the city where they sought refuge, the city which they sought to rescue, and the city on which they had pinned the last of their groundless hopes.

Having been denied a chance to calm his nerves, the messenger who had brought news of Albion's advance was the first to crack. "Mallerstang burns!" he screeched rabidly. "The Warden of Wrath has come!"

"The fires of Tiree have returned!" one of the soldiers cried, incited by the messenger's outburst. "These are not the days of Ibar, but of Gorsedd Cadell!"

"Death behind us, death before us!" howled another. "We will all of us be consumed!"

Osla reacted to the crisis with the instinct of a mother and the prudence of an elder. She knew that the full force of her army would be needed to save the King, if he was still alive; though she would not yet tell herself which king she hoped to save.

"No!" she pronounced definitively as she swung her horse to face the crowd, immediately quelling their unrest. "We shall *not* be consumed. We are the Army of the One Land!" She began ranging the front line with magisterial temerity. "Do you not know, men of Durdich, that this fire will purge our Land of its invaders – the pestilence of Albion, the locust-swarm of Aram, even the weeds and thorns among us who are unworthy of our holy inheritance? How happy it is that both our enemies have come to partake in this great purification!"

Osla beamed as she wheeled her steed, mocking death even as it came to claim its payment. "I tell you: it will be their end, not ours. Mark my words: this Land will spit them out, for they have broken the Culdee Covenant which was given to our fathers, the Keepers of Alba. Today, we protect the Keeper's legacy like a precious pearl bestowed on us from Heaven, like a sacred seed from which Heaven itself will grow."

Osla amplified to a militant climax. "Today *is* the day of Ibar, for we will make it so with the edges of our blades and the tips of our spears!" Raising her sword above her head, she released all of the trauma, shame, and anger which had been brewing in her sealed-up spirit since she was cut from her family, drowned in injustice, and leavened with the tenacity of imagination: "To the King!"

Mimicking their redoubtable leader, the beleaguered soldiers cheered back: "To the King!"

With Osla at their head, the army charged toward the city with fanatical valour. It soon became clear that the city was still being contested; along with the meagre force which had stayed behind, an unorganised but sizeable assemblage of immigrants was evidently opposing Albion's forces, which had already penetrated the city walls. The Land's Army entered with no resistance through the way they had come – the mighty Gate of Heaven and Earth, now charred to a cinder by the spreading flames. Without hesitation, Osla proceeded down the city's seventh artery towards its heart – the crucible of the conflict, the crux of destiny, and the cradle of a New World.

***

Carleol Square had become a gory pandemonium – an apocalypse of uncivilisation, where God had withdrawn his hand of mercy and extended his hand of judgement. To the acclamation of the Durdish residents, the Land's Army had initially repulsed the mercenaries of Andras Albion; but they were soon followed by the Aramite horde, whose hideous war-masks and harrowing scimitars betokened that the end had come. The battle had then disintegrated into an orgy of confusion, in which kingdom fought against kingdom, neighbour against neighbour, brother against brother, and the Devil took the foremost. All the while, the hellfire spread from the city walls, until the perimeter of the square itself was blazing like a pyre. This would be a fight to the death, for the victor as well as the vanquished; and yet the battle still raged, more fiercely even than the flames.

Bassien Dunragit entered the fray like one of the mighty men of old, the champions of renown immortalised in the epics and the ballads. He savoured the fear and the fury, and above all the fire; for such were the foundations of glory. His enemies had gathered for the contest to settle all contests, and for his life he would not balk at the invitation. He would honour the fallen fathers who watched him from the Lost Land, and who there prepared a place for him.

Yet one thing galled him: his real enemy was removed from the battle, watching from above. Even amid the carnage, Dunragit could not help but look to the Mast. Festooned with dangling rope, it stood like a fiery serpent untouched by the wreath of wrath, a beacon of healing for a world afflicted by its own disease. Its holiness had kept it whole, for it had raised up the First Son of the Last Father – the King of Righteousness, the King of Peace.

A sequence of unshakable truths now shook Dunragit to the core, for he had finally come to the core truth, the Truth beneath, above, and within all other truths. The Wood of Shamayim was a mere harbinger, an omen for the Oracle to induce its own fulfillment. Spellbound, he uttered aloud with sacred obsession:

> "The Silver Birch will be refined by the fire of Heaven;
>
> It will withstand the flame that consumes the dross of the earth.
>
> The Tree of Ibar will appear like a spire from Heaven;
>
> In a scorched place, it will draw the nations across the earth."

Dunragit was beyond himself, for his hopes and fears had coalesced in a heroic drama of destruction and salvation. Climbing the base of the Mast, he turned to the square and waved his ensanguined sword like one who is victorious even in death. "Hear me now, you oppressors! You tread on holy land, and you shall be thrown off, for Ibar's Tree is here! Our bonds shall be loosed, our yokes shall be undone, for now comes the resurrection of the One Land of Alba!"

Lusting for his own blood, Dunragit charged into the murderous debauch to seize his martyrdom, that he might be among the firstborn of the dead – that he might be set free by the Truth which had ever been proclaimed by the Land, but which had fallen on deaf ears until the trumpet call was heard even by those who already rested in the sacred soil. Yes, the fallow ground had finally been harrowed, and he would sow himself to reap its resurrection.

~ Chapter 61 ~

Urien reached the mouth of the valley before low eventide; but the light was immaterial, for this was a place that never saw the sun. Whereas the thick radiance of Melchizedek had filled him beyond what he could absorb, the deep darkness of Golgotha seemed to absorb whatever radiance was left within him, as if the marrow was being sucked out of his bones, the sinews of his flesh devoured while he still stood. The wind itself rushed into the emptiness, ushering him to empty himself. Urien cared not for his life, since he had already died; but Golgotha was a living death, an unthinkable, unspeakable rupture between one moment and the next, a torment which no man was ever meant to suffer.

When Urien stepped into the cleft, he found himself lapsing into a conscious fugue, in which he appeared as an artifact of his own demented mind. His body became a mere shell, his corporeal sensations untethered from any sense of self or singularity. The schism in the rock corresponded to a schism in his being; and the further he journeyed towards the crossroads of the kingdoms, the more alienated he became. It was like being swallowed by a circular serpent, which endlessly digests its prey into ever more elemental fragments but never grants it the relief of death.

In normal times, Golgotha was scrupulously overwatched from all sides; for although it was indomitably deep and impossibly steep, its narrowness placed the kingdoms in uncomfortably close proximity. In places, a man suspended in the crevasse would be capable of reaching both sides at once – although, among the scores of condemned men who had been cast into the chasm, none had succeeded in stopping their fall. Now that all of Abaddon was occupied by the Qa, the border stations were superfluous, and Urien had progressed along the fissure unchecked. Still, it was a full day before Urien reached the centre of Golgotha, for the path was rough, the light was dim, and the burden was heavy.

In the wilderness of Shur, Urien had relinquished the divine awareness of Gwydir Aspatria, the Ancient Way which kept the world alive. There, too, he had gazed in anguish at the unreachable light above, which seemed to banish him from all memory and all posterity. Yet the sheol did not compare to his present suffering, in which reality was not merely corrupted, but was corruption itself. This was not confinement, but exposure; not void, but torment; not darkness, but fire. It was the cesspool of a world which had forsaken its very life source, its very life force. It was the unholy axis of Tur, the malignant root from which the cancer of hatred had spread to choke off the peoples it divided. It was the edge of worlds.

~ Chapter 62 ~

Surrounded by a sea of stone, the Mast had initially been spared from the blaze which had already encompassed the square. Yet the dead wood was kindling, the dry rope tinder; and it was only a matter of time before a stray ember set the monument aflame, turning the criminal's prison into a heretic's stake. Owein looked on helplessly as the bloodbath around him was veiled by a cloud of fiery smoke, which grew ever thicker until he could feel it piercing his feet and stifling his lungs. He would have jumped to a merciful death if he were not still bound to the platform; yet there was mercy, for the lack of air set his mind at ease, as if he were already being laid to rest in the Garden of Shemesh.

Soothed by the delirium, the sacred sentience which he had received in the belly of the coracle seeped through his mind like oil. He saw his father in the temple of the Bramble, and there gave him water to drink; he saw his father in the sheol of Shur, and there gave him food to eat; and he saw his father in the pit of Golgotha, and there gave him his very self. His body was dry and broken like a shard of pottery returning to the furnace, to be rendered back into clay. Yet he was a living sacrifice, for his bier had become an altar, a table prepared for him in the presence of his enemies.

Owein saw Breaca, who had already crossed from life to life. Seeing with her own heart's eye, she must have awaited his arrival for years, even in the knowledge that their matrimony was no more than a dream.

Yes, Owein now understood, it was a dream, and no less than a dream; for it was the very dream which birthed creation, the eternal dream which he now dreamt. It was the Madness of the Sea, the affliction borne by those who know that the world is not as it should be – those who feel the world's bruises, who listen to its longings, who cannot help but see beyond the sea. Imprisoned in her sanctuary, Breaca had foreshadowed his captivity; now he would follow her into expiation, into absolution, into the Great Communion of flesh and blood, of body, spirit, soul.

Owein's final thought, like his first, was for his mother. After Urien had departed on his pilgrimage, it was believed that Coira, like Breaca, had lost her mind. Yes, Owein now understood, she did lose her mind – but only to gain the mind of redemption which he now possessed. It is the mind which is glimpsed in the last moments of life, when all meaning is illuminated and all vanity fades to nothing. It is the mind that empties itself to be ever filled, which humbles itself to be ever exalted. It is the mind that searches the mysteries of the ages to find what has been known since before the world began.

Owein heard his mother, as he often did, humming the simple hymn of Enoch's Prophecy. But this time, giddy with clarity, he let its liminal rhythm carry him to a time which he had long striven to forget, resentful of its hope and ashamed of its blissfulness. He could smell the wild vitality of the meadows where he used to play, building worlds and winning battles. He could taste the almond cakes that Coira used to bake, soused in milk and drizzled with honey. He could feel the heat of the hearth that Urien would stoke when the nights drew in and the vastness of the palace halls left him feeling all alone in an empty world.

Owein's sight returned to Mallerstang. He had never been more alone, for the Mast was becoming a hearth of its own. That relic from the blessed sea which told of a day when there will only be One Kingdom, One Land, One Way, was finally returning to its origin, to Heaven and to earth. Yet he could still hear his mother, who, having finished her melody, spoke to him the same words which she had spoken before he followed the Star of Esa into the Jacinth Sea:

> "The bridge, the breach; the door, the key;
> The thread through time, tied together
> In a circle. It ties together
> What is, what was, and what is to be.
> Under the sky, above the sea
> It lies in perfect symmetry.
> It splits the oceans, joins the lands –
> At the edge of worlds, Langstrath stands."

Chapter 63

Nana always knew, didn't she?

Mungo stood in the Garden of Shemesh, by himself but not alone. He contemplated the acorn in his hand, which he presented to himself as one might present a wedding ring to one's beloved. It was his father's burden, and his grandfather's; it was his mother's vision, and his grandmother's. Now the burden would be laid down, and the vision would thus come true. For with its sacred seal and its message of truth, it was Osla's letter, ready to be opened. And in the fullness of time, it would be opened; it would give birth to the Great Oak which it already carried in its womb.

Mungo had already dug the hole which would hold the grain of truth, yet which could never truly hold it. As he sowed the righteous seed, he prayed the seminal verse of Enoch's Prophecy, just as his Nana used to, just as he used to do at the well by his home in Hartsop:

> "The Diadem interred in earth
> The Cornerstone raised up to Heaven;
> What is above and what is below
> Will be rebirthed as one expression
> Of perfect love, its perfect flow,
> And out of love the New World will grow."

***

Aelhairn Urien now passes out of this tale; for he passes to Shailana, the Holy Land; to Shailoh, its Holy City; and to Shainor, its Holy

Mountain. There he crosses the rivers that water the world; and at the summit of Earth, at the foundation of Heaven, He offers up the Cornerstone, so that what is above and what is below, what is before and what is after, what is beyond and what is within, may be all in all.

> For the Wisdom is above all things
> And by the Wisdom all things exist.
> For the Glory is before all things
> And of the Glory all things witness.
> For the Spirit is beyond all things
> And in the Spirit all things consist.

Some believe that he was caught up to Elana, the Highest Heaven, to the very House of Elai, and thus what he beheld and what he became cannot even be told in the words of mortal men, who are but dust. Yet what no eye can see, what no ear can hear, what no hand can touch — that which we have seen, that which we have heard, and that which we have touched — of that we testify:

> "The King of Peace will come again,
> Back from Shailoh He will come.
> To Water's End His Son will come,
> To make the World new again."

THE END.

~ Epilogue ~

Dahaka savoured the swell of the sea. He let it massage his memory and enliven his imagination. He wondered what Qahal was like.

The sea seemed endless, and perhaps it was; perhaps Qahal lay beyond eternity. He would reach it nonetheless, whether through life or through death, for he had sailed too far to turn back. His heart was already there; it had always been there.

He never dreamed that he would see this day, which had been foreseen by his fathers before him. They had been the least of the men of Tur, and unto them had been done the worst. They had cursed the sea, for it had separated them from their homeland, from their heartland.

Yet Dahaka would bless the sea, for he could do no other. These were the days of the New Men; the New World had come.

~ Appendices ~

~ *The Seven Winds* ~

Yom Matzot	Elyon's Whisper
Yom Shavout	Elyon's Breath
Yom Pesach	Elyon's Cry
Yom Kippur	Elyon's Song
Yom Sukkot	Elyon's Word
Yom Teruah	Elyon's Trumpet
Yom Katzir	Elyon's Laughter

The Great Oak – the Standard of Rheged

The Birch of Ibar – the Standard of Durdich

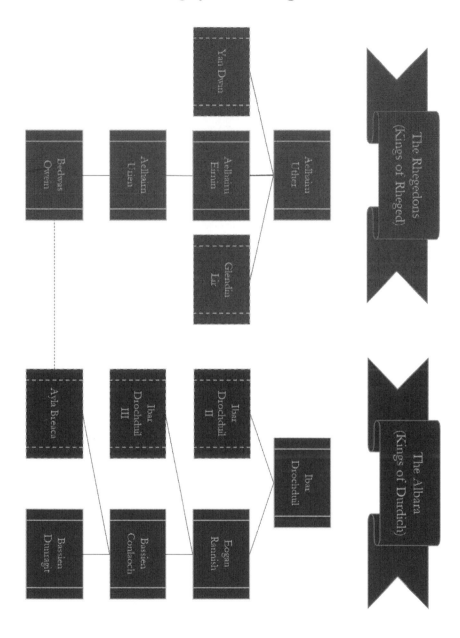

~ *Tur* ~

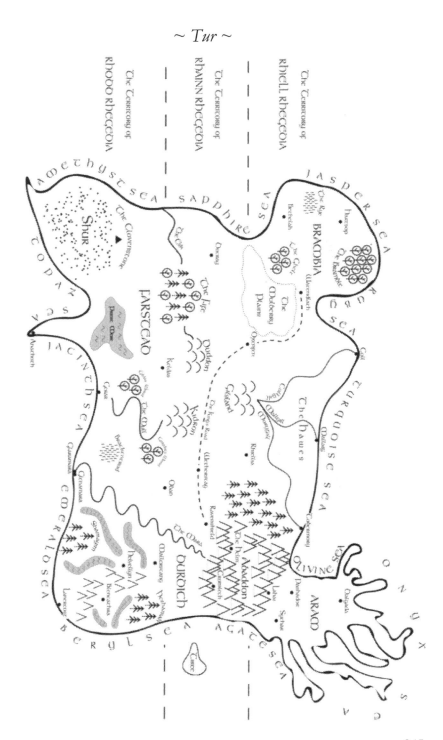

Printed in Great Britain
by Amazon